The Lucky Charm of Major Bessop

Reviews of Tom Hubbard's recent Work

On the novel *Marie B.* (Ravenscraig Press, 2008)

"Our tat-crammed bookshelves are so depressing [but] thanks to Ravenscraig Press for Tom Hubbard's *Marie B.* [...] recapturing the young Russian painter Marie Bashkirtseff and the world of French realism [...] defending the classics against an anti-culture of commercialised drivel."

--- CHRISTOPHER HARVIE in his 'round-up' of 2009,
Sunday Herald (Glasgow)

On the poetry collection *Chagall Winnocks* (Grace Note Publications, 2011)

"At stake is not just parity of poetic esteem for Scots but the status of the spoken and written word in general."

--- MICHAEL KERRIGAN in the *Scotsman*

On the pamphlet poetry collection *The Nyaff* (Windfall Books, 2012)

"sharp, funny and sly"

--- MICHELLE SMITH
in *Sphinx: Chapbook poetry review*

On the poetry collections *Chagall Winnocks* and *Parapets and Labyrinths* (Grace Note Publications, 2011 & 2013)

"The wandering scholar is a great European tradition and Scotland has had her share, poets, singers, the restless and endlessly curious, travelling workers in literature, language and the arts. Among the most distinctive riches yielded by this tradition, Tom Hubbard's poems are evocative encounters with places, people, political and personal states, that range across Europe and history, centred in his own Scottish sensibility, but receptive to, exploring and describing, different nations, artists and cultures."

--- ALAN RIACH, poet and Professor of Scottish
Literature at the University of Glasgow

The Lucky Charm of Major Bessop

A Grotesque Mystery of Fife

Tom Hubbard

GRACE NOTE PUBLICATIONS

The Lucky Charm of Major Bessop
This edition published 2014 by
Grace Note Publications C.I.C.
Grange of Locherlour,
Ochtertyre, PH7 4JS,
Scotland

books@gracenotereading.co.uk
www.gracenotepublications.co.uk

ISBN 978-1-907676-48-2

First published in 2014

Three of the poems have appeared in *Four Fife Poets* (Aberdeen University Press) and *Scottish Poetry in Translation* (Glasgow University postgraduates)

Author photo back cover: Kenny Munro
Cover designed by Grace Note Publications.

FOR TESSA RANSFORD
*She has changed the direction
of many lives and arts*

CONTENTS

PART ONE

A HALF-CENTURY, ACROSS

1

THE BIG HOOSE: 2012, 1962

Halfway down the winding drive to Mauletoun House, the stranger might pause to take in the view.

A good swatch of the Howe of Fife can be enjoyed here. Robert Louis Stevenson would refer to the 'bleak fertility' of this region. Quite so. These fields have always been abundant, unlike that terrain – much further north-east – which had to be howked sweatily over many years before it could yield anything worth the eating. No: here in this peninsular county, which has kept its own counsel from the rest of Scotland, the stranger feels both oddly welcome and kept at a distance.

What does that matter, though, when she can look across to the twin summits of the Lomonds, even shielding her eyes a little during that hot unaccustomed summer.

It is by no means the best view. From the stark parish church, outlined at the top of the brae, it's much more dramatic. The stranger, though, might not be able to expunge her prejudices anent such a Calvinistic barn. (If she bothered to peek through the latticed window, she might find the interior not unwelcome, the sunlight generous upon the white walls and columns, the pews and pulpit shiny from local bottoms and lurid sermons.)

For all that, though, she has chosen a fine view. With a smile, she might well admit that it is indeed a braw view.

Who couldn't fling their arms wide, to embrace everything and everyone before them, like a national liberator during his country's and his own rehabilitation?

A lot of folk couldn't.

Especially hereabouts.

It takes a great deal of history to make a people cautious and alert. At the entrance to the drive, there is the incongruously English-y lodge to one side, roses tumbling over the trellis; on the other, near-hidden in the undergrowth, rises the ancient tower once briefly inhabited by Scotland's bonny fechter, Sir William Wallace, shortly before his betrayal to the Sassenachs. The country road passes this entrance at the point known as the clachan of Lettermuchill. A clachan – neither village, nor hamlet, but a clachan. A triangle of rough lawn, cottages behind with red postbox inserted into their wall. Two burial grounds, one by the tower for the lairds and their progeny; the other by the farmtrack leading to a deserted quarry with the dreich muir beyond, and inhabited by generations of the indigenous - as well as by a few exotic incomers whose names ended in –ski. Every now and then someone still opens the rusty gate, straightens a fallen jar of flowers by a grave, places a small flag of horizontal white and red.

Let the stranger take a few steps further down the brae, let her imagine herself at that spot almost exactly fifty years earlier, and she might not be unduly intimidated by the appearance of a man and a woman in late middle age. At just that time, this couple would be standing on the little brig which carries the drive between a line of oaks, across a pappling burn, to the Big Hoose, the ancestral home of the Earls of Mauletoun and Rossie. (There came here, at an even earlier date, the ancestor-hunting father of a famous American architect, intent on visiting his distant aristocratic cousin.)

The man and woman of 1962 would have walked the few steps from their wing of the mansion and leaned on the parapet of the brig, seeming to be lost in some private reverie. One would like to think that, if they had suddenly looked up in the direction of the twenty-first century stranger, they would have hailed her with a friendly wave.

They were the Colonel and his wife.

2

BILLY TORRANCE REMEMBERS

Oh I know why ma parents sent me to that place – get me oot o the way so's they could have their wee orgies in megalosuburbia.

I couldnae wait to get the hell oot o Mauletoun Hoose. OK it's full o history but it's no the kind o history I like – I go for artists and composers hingin oot in the nineteenth century by European lakes – and in any case the past at Mauletoun, the past that matters, had faded lang ago.

No, when I was a laddie there, it was just all post-post-Suez mustiness, late Harold Macmillan era withoot Harold Macmillan's style. Oh I mind when the music teacher, he took us for choir, and he telt us that Vaughan Williams wis his musical grandfaither, and I wis fair impressed – but I later found oot that what he meant was he was taught by a prof at St Andrews University who'd been taught by RVW himsel. Still it wis a wee island o civilisation in that philistocratic dump o a school.

Mrs Malory – Cathy Malory, the Colonel's wife that wis the 'matron' or head nurse in the school, oh she wis a real sweetie. Mair o a mother ti me than my mother ever was. Reminded me o my granny a bit, younger version, miner's daughter where granny was miner's wife. Common as muck, like us – no, that's no fair. She wisnae common, juist doun ti earth like, but wi an indulgent smile that let ye know she knew that you knew what your limits should be. Still ye'd sometimes get the feelin she'd let ye off wi murder and sure there were an awfy lot o people at Mauletoun ye'd want to murder.

Oh Billy Torrance, she'd say, *ye're a wicked boy. I'll have to send you to Captain Wilkie, he'll sort you out.*

And she just laughed.

One day at breakfast I wis scrapin the green stuff off o ma bread and Burt, wee Burtie we called him, he comes up and sits opposite me. Oh no, I thought, cos wee Burtie he smelt like all the human farts of the world at once.

Hey Burtie, says I, *want some o ma bread? I'll ping it at ye.*

I'd rather not, says he.

I'd rather not. He said that rather a lot.

Poor auld Burtie.

It wasnae a nice way to go, the way he went.

Anyways, there he is, I continue to offer him a slice of bread (unscraped), but he'd rather not, and I'd rather not have him opposite me. But something in me – where in me? Not in my balls, that's for sure – pities the poor bugger. Voices assail him from all sides, and I keep my mouth shut. I don't want the other boys to notice I'm there: forlorn hope.

Ooooh Miss Torry – that's one o them addressin me

– You don't want to chat up Burtie, you don't know what ye'd catch off him.

Burtie! Burtie! Dirty Burtie! It becomes a shout. *Give me your answer do. I'm half crazy over the love of you.*

He should be in a loony bin.

Mind you, when they're tauntin him, it kind of deflects attention off o me, not that they bother me much to be honest. I'm a kind o pariah, being the Überpoof as it were.

He should be locked up with man-eating rats.

He's not a man though.

The rats would have to be real men, to put up with the stink and want to eat him. Little wog, woggie Burt.

That's how they'd go on. They'd tie him up in a moment behind the pavilion, if they could (why couldn't they, if it comes to that), and barbecue the bugger. No that they'd eat him theirsels. They're no men, no the men I go for anyways.

It's infantile, the way they go on … the way they *went* on. It wis a long time ago. And, er, they, we, *were* infants then. What are they doing now? No that I care. Investment managers, I suppose, whatever that is, or sportsmen (probably in the news, if I deigned to follow the news), politicians … so borin. Spiritually they probably stink far worse than wee Burtie did at Mauletoun Hoose.

The crimes of their boyhood they will continue, more or less, into their adulthood. When they snap their fingers, batches o unemployed keelies will shiver and rot under a bridge, Africans will be poisoned by their products.

Shits they were then, shits they will be now. And far worse than then.

No that I care, to be honest.

Burtie? Oh yes, Burtie.

He has – had – a head like a pear, a pear that's got aa squished and flattened at the bottom. It gien him a permanently mournful look. His skin wis orange, a yellowy orange, no healthy. He'd been long in the sun, though he didnae have the complexion to make that attractive. His parents wis tea-planters outby Ceylon or whitever they call it nou. He never saw his mummy and daddy from one end o the year to the other, did oor Burtie. In the dorm I'd hear him variously playin wi himsel, pishin his bed (oh ay, he added that to his list o fragrances) and greetin for his mammy. Often someone would throw a slipper at him and that shut him up - for a while – until the next slipper crash-landed on him. By the morning his bed would be surrounded by heaps o slippers. I'm no exaggeratin, much.

In wunderschönen Monat Mai
Als alle Knospen sprangen

I used to listen ti that a lot. Still do, in ma wee flat outby Byres Road … still listen to it on that auld Fischer-Dieskau LP. There isnae a scratch on it. I took care o that. My idiot faither wouldae binned it if I hadnae hidden it when I wis hame. That man wis a barbarian.

Anyway, there I was, in the music room at Mauletoun, singin along, accompanyin the greater man – I've got a pretty good voice myself, ye know (of course ye know), and nae wonder wi Fischer-Dieskau as a mentor.

I wis enjoyin my all-too-transitory period o culture before the bloody bell rang. We were ti heid up the brae, for chapel this Sunday wis ti be in Lettermuchill Parish Church, bi-Gode. Bi-Gode indeed. The meenister, the Reverend Hamish McClutchie (or something like that) – I mean, he wis awful, awfy. Awfissimo. Fair hammerin the pulpit and bangin on aboot Predestination, or mebbe it wis Procrastination. Predestination is aboot not bein able to do tomorrow what you should have done yesterday, procrastination wis not bein able to do tomorrow what had already been decided for ye yesterday, or was it the other round?

Summer mornings wis the worst. Ye're in that aesthetically-underperformin kirk, no a Renaissance fresco in sight, the Reverend waving his arms aboot, and the sweat pourin aff o him – he smoked cigars before and efter the service, would ye believe – oh the mingled reek, it wis worse even than wee Burtie, who of course wis there to make his own contribution in that muckle box of delights.

Oh ay – and who wis it conducted us there and back, in the school's finest military style? Nane other than Mikie Bessop, Major Mikie Bessop. A braw man, oh a real braw man, I'll gie him that. But the glower on him would fix ye, pin ye to the wall, leave ye there. The cauld grue o his eyes. *He* should have been in the pulpit, no the Reverend Hamish McHushie. Major Mikie Bessop would have ye over the charcoal-burner in no time.

Mind you, the boys as I say made it hell enough for Master Andrew Burt, wee Burtie. He didnae deserve to go like that, in spite o smellin like all the human farts o the world at once.

3

THE MALORYS RECEIVE A GUEST: 1962

Colonel Malory looked up from his paper, took off his glasses, rubbed his eyes, brushed the paper from his lap.

His wife, Cathy, asked him if he was feeling all right. Her expression displayed concern for the man she loved, together with her professional attentiveness to a patient.

'Yes, yes. It's just that I can't get angry any more. Even with this – ' He pointed to an article in the paper.

'Ye're not an angry kind of man, Pete.' Mrs Malory smiled, gazed at her husband with amused affection.

'No, but I sometimes feel I should be. And yet sometimes I am. Poor little Andy Burt – '

Mrs Malory was startled. 'Ye don't get angry at him?'

'No, no, not at him.'

'The wee soul.'

'It was one Sunday, I was on duty. I took the boys for their walk. We were having a good time, me striding through that little wood, that … "den" (as folk – as you - call it) below Lettermuchill, and I'd raise my stick to point out the gorse-bushes along the way.'

'Oh ay, the whins, just by the burn.'

'Yes, yes – as you say. And you know what it's like, the usual, we only have them for a few years at most, but they become our kids, our bairns if you like – ' He stopped himself.

Cathy gently touched his hand.

'Well, Strang senior was asking me a question about the geology of the den. Bright lad, Strang. I've high hopes for him. Could be Head Boy before long, 'cording to higher authority. Once offered him extra tuition, soon realised he should be tutoring me!'

The Colonel laughed, but his look darkened.

'Then I heard screams. It was little Andy. I should have been more watchful – as if I'd forgotten all my training out East. A couple of the boys – I won't say who: perhaps I should.'

'I can guess.'

'They'd got hold of an old door – big thing, the wood rotten but so thick it was hard enough – down by that metal bridge it was, and they'd pushed Andy under it. They were about to jump on it. I raised my stick, I'd have thrashed them … then I remembered my training, you might say.

'They could have killed the boy, Cathy!'

Mrs Malory poured some tea for her husband.

'Ye never told me about this …'

'No, Cathy, I didn't. I should have done. Should've let you deal with the culprits in your way, and the headmaster in his. It was only afterwards I realised the seriousness of it all. I told Strang to deal with it, level-headed lad that he is.

'Am I losing my touch?

'I suppose I've seen too much of the savagery of war. It hadn't prepared me for the savagery of peace.' Colonel Malory pointed to the article in his newspaper. 'This fellow – politician, journalist, don't know what he is, says we should go into Kazimiria because they nationalised their oil wells, protect our interests, challenge the Soviets, strategic reasons as he calls 'em – what does he know? Kazimiria was never part of our Empire. Even the Americans don't want to get involved!

'But you know what I think. Chaps in these colonies, they come back from some bally desk job, they know it all, get some damned pundit down in London on their side – oh God, if they only knew what war was really like. And now, these days, that bomb – oh no – '

'Drink up your tea, Pete.'

'Sorry, Cathy. I'm going on. I'm getting on. Need to retire, tend a nice little garden, cottage up by Wester Cadham. Would be ideal.'

'I cannae retire yet. I'm needit here.'

'Yes, yes, and so am I, it seems. They're our boys, then we lose them.'

Cathy laughed. 'Then we get another batch of the wee buggers.'

She suggested that during the 'vac' ('as you call it, Pete, you and thae ither English bodies here!') – they should look up their nephew Neil and his wife in Amsterdam. Had two bonny lassies, they'd be stretching now. Need to spend time with them while they were still bairns.

'Ay, bairns' – and here Peter lingered on the 'r' in bairns. It was his turn to tease his wife, or 'bother' her as she put it. And he lingered on the 'r' in bother, too, for good measure.

Colonel Malory smiled, picked up his copy of *The Times*, folded it and elegantly placed it in the waste-paper basket.

'Wee Andy Burt,' said Mrs Malory. 'We'll need to keep watching out for him. And my new start, the lassie from America, she can help.' The couple heard steps outside in the corridor: someone was approaching their flat.

'Whatever we can do for Andy, we'll do it,' said the Colonel. 'He's an "Oriental" – a bit like me. I knew his parents' type out East – vulgar, neglectful. Their children always need that protective eye … '

'Ay, and we'll need to keep an eye on that Captain Wilkie.'

'You've never liked Norrie Wilkie, Cathy.'

'The brute.'

There was a knock on the door. The Colonel opened it. A slim young man stood there, as if at attention. Darkly handsome, hooded eyes, determined expression. Not yet thirty, but with an air of being much older and much younger.

'Mike – Michael,' said the Colonel. 'Nice to see you. Do come in, my dear chap. Have a drop of Talisker – oh, I forgot, you don't.'

The young man saluted; the older man smiled in return.

'Sir, I need to report to you,' said Major Michael Bessop. 'Matter of some urgency.'

'Yes, yes, quite, quite. Sit you down, my dear chap. Cathy will bring you some tea.'

'Good morning, matron - Mrs Malory.'

'Oh hello to ye, Michael. Make yersel at home.'

'Awfully kind of you, Mrs Malory, but I'm afraid I can't stay long. On duty today, sir.'

The Colonel had pulled out a chair for the young man.

'Well, well, whatever you please, Mike – Michael. I'm not your commanding officer.'

Colonel Malory smiled. Major Bessop didn't.

'Righty-ho, Michael, old chap. Let's have it.'

'It's Captain Wilkie.'

Cathy Malory looked to heaven: heaven had no answer.

'I feel he's challenging my authority, sir,' the young man resumed. 'I impose a punishment on a boy, he makes it more severe.'

'Surprise, surprise,' said Cathy Malory, then realised that she was speaking out of turn.

'Michael – do please sit down, my boy – have you spoken to the headmaster about this?'

'No sir. The headmaster is a civilian. I do not feel that he understands the nature of discipline.'

Colonel Malory frowned.

'Neither does Captain Wilkie, it seems,' he remarked, with a feigned nonchalance. 'But Dr Baxendale is still the headmaster.'

Michael Bessop stared, as if he could not quite understand.

Colonel Malory smiled.

'Dr Baxendale's not your commanding officer either. But he's your boss, he's my boss, Mrs Malory's boss, Captain Wilkie's boss. If you're worried about something, you must go to him before you come to me.'

'Sir!' The Major saluted again. The Colonel made a light hand gesture, as if to ward off, as tactfully as he could, the unwanted assumption of subordination.

'Now, Michael my boy, sit with us for a while, my dear chap, enjoy some more of this excellent tea, then report to ... see Harry Baxendale in his study. That's the proper procedure,' he added with a grin, 'according to regulations.'

Major Bessop tried awkwardly to salute, and even more awkwardly took his seat and sipped his tea.

'By the by,' said the Colonel. 'When does this punishment come into effect?'

'This evening, sir, just before prep.'

'And may I ask who is Captain Wilkie's intended victim?'

'Burt, sir.'

The Malorys exchanged quick looks.

'Then finish your tea, Michael,' said the Colonel, 'and go straight to Dr Baxendale. And – yes, you should tell him you've spoken to me. Harry Baxendale will put a stop to this. I'm sure of it.'

Cathy Malory stepped closer to her husband, placed a hand on his shoulder.

'And thank you for ... reporting this, Michael,' said Colonel Malory.

'Sir.'

This time the salute was a successful one, but the Colonel again gently waved it away. Meanwhile his wife was contemplating how she might explain this and that to her new 'start', the lassie from the American South.

4

THE SOUTHERN NURSE
SETTLES IN: 1962

September 21, -

Man, I'm pooped.

Bin here a week now, the kids have arrived, just about gittin to understand the little critters. The adults? Still hafta meet em, most on em; like the kids, they come by train – they all come by train here, with them cute cars they have that smell funny – 'cept cars is what they drives, they call the railroad cars 'carriages'.

Classy, eh?

Yup, it's classy here, and kinda weird.

Man, I'm pooped. But I thought I oughter git back to my journal. What I'm gonna write, though, I don't think I'm gonna show it to the folks back home, I'd be lynched man.

Durin the summer I went to this Journal Writin class at WASUA – that's Western Altawba State University at Albemarle to you Brits, but a lotta folks think WASUA's an Injun word and think it should have a name that could be pronounced easy like Billy Graham Bible College. Gimme a break! Yup we're in that part of the country, southern Baptists spawnin like frogs in Covington Creek.

Anyways, I'm at WASUA, and the professor's kinda cute, I seem to be lucky enrollin in the classes with cute professors, and this woman she comes up to me, 30, bout ma age, she's recruitin for the Klan.

Well, I'm a friendly kinda gal, even when I'm with nuts, so I hears her out.

She's real heavy though, wants me to sign up. 'Cordin to her, them nigguhs is gittin kinda uppity them days.

'Us white folks has gotta stick togethuh.'

How do I reply to that? Only one way man.

'What makes you think I'm white, Lurleen? I'm half Cherokee.'

Jee-zus she looks at me likes she coulda blasted ma tits off. Preferably slowly.

Some o them white supremacists though, they know their Civil War history (the ones that can read, the others git it at their grandpappy's knee) and o course there was Injuns on the Confederate side. Injuns helpin to keep the white race pure. I mean, hello?

Anyways.

Thing you notice here, is how quiet it is. Cathy, the old lady, reminds me of my ma cept she speaks funny, she's put me in a room in the West Wing. *West* Wing – said she thought it'd be nearer home for me than the East Wing. Ain't that neat?

At nights, all I can hear is the owls. Kinda creepy, but hey man, I like all them ghost legends, and this is Scotland.

One of my great-great-great-great grandpappies, he come from Scotland.

Most on em here, though, ain't so much Scottish as British. It takes time to figger out all them accents. Cathy, she ain't British, she got a brogue, a nice lilt, though a lotta her words, I hafta say to her *Pardon me*? But she's patient, real patient. She'd calm the winds if she could, and it's real windy here. Wooooooh it is. Ain't at all like Altawba, even high up in the Smoky Mountains.

Doc Baxendale, the principal, only here they calls em headmaster, he's real nice, always puffin on his pipe, takes it outa his mouth to say somethin wise. Always quotin Shakespeare – ain't that neat? You can tell why he's the boss, kinda quiet strength about him.

And of course the Colonel. You can tell he was a beautiful man in his time, still is if you go for the very mature types. Some o my girlfriends, it's the guys over seventy they get the hots for. I don't like that. They could be their daddies, man! (In the Smoky Mountains, some on em *are* their daddies.)

He ain't like how we think of a Colonel back home. You know, like in grey uniform on a hoss, leadin Johnny Reb agin the damYankees, or settin on his deck with his mint julep, you know that kinda stuff?

The real gen'leman type, with his goatee beard, sellin ya fried chicken. Y'know, all that typical Southern shit.

No: Colonel Malory he's a different kinda gen'leman, and I mean a real gen'leman, nice manners. Silver hair, face all brown, not like a nigro but you could tell he's bin out in one of them British colonies, long afore he settled here with Miz Cathy.

The kids? None o em fat, though most on em musta come from classy families with butlers and You-rang-sir stuff like ya see in them British movies? Cathy, she says she tries to be careful what the kids eat, she ain't in charge of the kitchen exac'ly, Mrs Makarowski is, but Cathy knows howta exert authority in her unassumin way. And man, I know it – the way she puts me right when I say or do somethin dumb.

Yeah, Mrs Makarowski – here they pronounce the Polak names different, she ain't Mrs MakarOUWski, she's Mrs MakarAWEski. Awesome. And some on em put an F after the AWE. MakarAWEFski. Weird.

Anyways – kids back home, they're different. They hafta roll themselves into school, their heads is kinda squished into their bodies, their legs can't neither walk nor even waddle – all them folds of flesh, they don't wash in between and under, so all the crud collects and can git gangrenous, you hafta act quickly on them kids or they're goners. I know, I'm a kids' nurse, that's why I'm here (though heck knows kids is mostly a pain in the butt). But, yeah, there ain't none o them problems with obesity here. Back in Altawba, all the kids eats is burgers and home fries. Give em anythin else, biscuits and gravy, and they stink out the joint. Me, I like to stick to ma grits, it's the good ole Southern way. Hey, can you git grits here?

September 23, -

Followed one of the trails, just beyond the 'lodge', to an old quarry and, on the moors just beyond, a cluster of weird outcrops formin a nat'ral citadel – remindin me o the Cullowhee Knobs, where a Cherokee Chief gave himself up to the Great Spirit. Cathy says ya can see a giant face on the quarry, but I couldn't – tho maybe I'm expectin the profile o that there Chief and he ain't there.

September 24, -

Two other adults, teachers, met em both over the weekend. One I don't like, one I mebbe do.

Captain Wiklie – have I spelt his name right? – man, is he fierce, round red face, looks like he could explode like a balloon filled with raw steaks, if ya said the wrong thing. Then he'll smile at ya, real sly, like them limeys they always has as villains in the movies, tries to be all friendly-like but you hafta be on your guard. In the Navy. Man, if he was on a ship in the Atlantic he'd sure scare the shit outa Mistah Kroosschoff's Commie dudes.

I can't understand a friggin word he says.

And Major Bessop. Gee I'd sure rather call him Mike. Will he let me? Anyways, that's enough for now. Sure thing, I'll have a lot to say about him as Swell Ole Time Goes a-Dancin On.

He's like one of em tall trees up the Smokies. Takes a long time to reach em and they're tough to climb.

And man is he cute.

5

KINRIK; SCRAPBOOK

Lindores ti Bruntisland,
 Tayport ti Longannet;
Ilk Jean maun hae her Jamie,
 Ilk Jock his Janet.

Elie ti Benarty,
 Dunbog ti Cullaloe,
There ye'll find some snod wee neuk
 Ti lie doun wi yer jo.

Letham ti Dunfermline,
 Glen ti Glen,
Fields and foliage
 Burgeon, ripen,
Blebo Craigs ti Kelty,
 Strathmiglo ti Raith;
May your sons and dochters
 Defeat your daith.

Young, you sclimmed the Paps o Fife,
Placed chuckies on the cairns;
Lang or the hinner-end o life,
Lat ilk guidman wi his guidwife
Return here wi their bairns.

('Kinrik')

EXTRACTS FROM THE (DAMAGED) SCRAPBOOKS OF MR WILLIAM TORRANCE OF ADAM SMITH SQUARE, HILLHEAD, GLASGOW, RECONSTRUCTED (AS FAR AS POSSIBLE) AND EDITED BY MS MURIEL REDBURN, GUSHETNEUK PLACE, RUBISLAW, ABERDEEN, DURING 2012, PRIOR TO VISITING PROFESSOR NEIL MALORY GOMSHALL OF AMSTERDAM

MALORY, Peter Anthony. Born --- 190-, Westcott, Surrey. Educ.: Albury Military Staff College; Cobbett College, Cambridge, B.A. (Upper Second) in History, 193-. Army service in India and Burma; Distinguished Service Medal (D.S.M), 194-. Associate of the Royal Scottish College of Historians (A.R.S.C.H), Fellowship candidature pending. Teacher of History, Geography and English, Mauletoun School, Fife, 1957-65, Crockarkie College, 1964-5. Spouse: Catherine Sheila McPhail, S.R.N. [State Registered Nurse].

[Untraced reference book, believed to be published c. 1977 – MR]
[Handwritten note in margin: 'This record is believed to be an incomplete account of Peter Malory's career – WT']

WILKIE, Norman ('Norrie') Alexander. Born --- 191-, Port Edgar, Midlothian. Educ.: Craigarter School; Firth of Clyde Naval Academy. Naval service in the Mediterranean; Distinguished Service Medal (D.S.M.), 194-. Teacher of Physics, Chemistry and Mathematics, Mauletoun School (later Crockarkie College), 195- - 67. Senior Lecturer, Firth of Clyde Naval Academy, 1967-71, 1972-76. Spouse: Molly Mathieson.
[Same reference book – MR]

BESSOP, Richard Michael Mountclifton. Born 193-, Wellington, Shropshire. Educ.: Stockbridge School, North Riding, Yorkshire; University of Stratford: B.A. (Hons.) in English. Army service: [print obscured and indecipherable at this point], invalided (?) [indecipherable] Royal Hibernian [indecipherable] injury (?) [the rest of the entry is obscured; I have been unable to infer the rest. The typography does suggest, however, that this is from the same reference book, and we know that Major Bessop taught at Mauletoun sometime during the early 1960s and left for reasons that are as yet not entirely clear to me at this early stage in my research, though the implications, to say the least, are sinister. – MR]

PUBLIC NOTICES

JOHN ANTONELLI and NICOL TULLOCH of ----, Hillhead, Glasgow, are delighted to announce that they entered into Civil Partnership at Botanic Terrace Registry Office, on June 25, 20-. They wish to thank their dear friend Billy Torrance for introducing them to each other and for subsequent emotional and practical support.

[Handwritten note, by WT, in margin:
Hillhead Herald, July 1, 20-.]

6

LEARNED CONVERSATION: 1963

Flossie was pawing her master for a walk, so Dr Henry Baxendale picked up his tobacco pouch and matches. Briefly – it was often briefly – he took his pipe from his mouth.

'Floss, old Floss. Always the boss.'

And he quickly replaced the pipe in its usual position, puffing away as he attached the dog's lead to her collar. At the main entrance he exchanged his suedes for a formidable pair of boots, picked up his stick, waved it playfully at Strang senior, who was heading to the pavilion for some cricket practice.

'Jolly good,' said the Headmaster to the future Head Boy.

As he turned the corner of the East Wing, Peter Malory opened the door and stepped out.

'Well met by daylight, Peter,' said Dr Baxendale, cheerily. 'Join us on our walk? What d'ye think, Floss? May he join us?'

Flossie squealed with delight as Colonel Malory rubbed her ears.

'Good idea, Harry. I was needing a breather. And the sky's clear.'

'Until the welkin doth ope its chaps. "Fair is foul, and foul is fair".'

Baxendale's verbal tics normally amused the Colonel but he remained sombre and distracted.

'You should teach me some of these "snatches of old tunes" you've been researching, Peter. Y'know, all that rustic lore of this land of heather and haggis hereabout. On which, how's that Fellowship thesis of yours going, old chap? Molto lentissimo? Ah, well, "creeps in this petty pace from day to day". Was glad to get my D.Phil. behind me – on Shakespeare's diphthongs, if I recall aright. Something like that. Sounds obscure, and it was bloody boring. Fell asleep writing it; pitied m' supervisor. Cathy well?'

Mrs Malory had been a little poorly of late.

'Yes, yes, Harry,' muttered Peter, absently. 'Nothing she can't treat herself. Dr Davidson thinks she's fitter than some of the boys. My own diagnosis – no, that matters little …'

'I know what's troubling you, Peter, No need for it. Had a quiet word with Wilkie. That young fella, the Bessop man, he came to see me.'

'Yes, yes, Harry, I told him to. It puts me in an embarrassing situation, the way he acts as if we were both still in the army.'

'Conscientious chap. Needs to relax, "be a child o' the time".'

'He was genuinely worried about Burt – '

'Needs to get himself a girl. D'ye know if there's one on the horizon? "The man that hath a tongue, I say, is no man, / If with his tongue he cannot win a woman."'

Malory gazed awkwardly at the statue of Venus in the formal garden. The tenth Earl had brought it from Italy and it looked incongruous in its north Fife setting.

'Naughty Floss.'

Baxendale smiled indulgently at the dog, who had just relieved herself at one of the two small houses at the far end of the garden.

'She hath opened her waters by the wall of Mr Anderson's gazebo. After this, can't see him translating any more dog stories into Latin.'

Malory smiled, if a little reluctantly.

'Peter' – Baxendale suddenly faced the Colonel – 'd'ye think Bessop's after that American girl?'

'Gayle? Oh no. I can't see it.'

Malory permitted himself a faint chuckle at the thought.

'No … oh … but – ' Baxendale seemed, for once, off

his guard. 'But – she's after him, d'ye think?'

Malory couldn't offer an opinion.

'Got her clutches into him? Peter, these Yanks!'

Baxendale waved his pipe, and was uncharacteristically slow in replacing the stem in his mouth.

'Never gone for them m'self. American women. Too loud. Engage the tongue all too precipitately – ' Baxendale tapped his forehead. 'Alas, this department here is rarely invited to witness the utterance, far less to direct it.'

Malory smiled.

'Peter, old chap: don't you worry about young Master Burt,' Baxendale placed a brotherly hand on Peter's shoulder. 'Flossie doesn't, and she's wiser than the rest of us, save your Cathy.' He added, more to himself than to Peter, that he hoped the boys would not pick up 'that frightful accent', or anything else, from the 'Southern nurse'.

It was February. A late winter chill was offset by the sun's rays, brightening a little the austerity of the long straight walk to the southern lodge. According to Baxendale, as he waved his stick and puffed on his pipe, there was an 'unnerving parallelism' in these lines of stark trees on either side of the track, and those boggy stretches over there seemed to threaten the unwary who might stray from the path.

'As well we have little Floss to guide us safely on our perilous journey.'

At the lodge, they turned back.

'Harry – ' Malory checked himself as a boy appeared from Mr Anderson's gazebo, having been receiving extra Latin tuition. 'Headmaster.'

Baxendale looked up, hoping to be ready with an answer to whatever was coming.

'Headmaster, I just feel we should be extra vigilant. I blame myself for not seeing warning signs earlier. If it wasn't Burt, it could be another boy at risk.'

'Peter, the Mauletoun tradition will win through. I'll address the boys on this at assembly. Now, you and Cathy, both of you come up to my rooms for a drop or two. This evening – you're both free? We'll discuss it together, as friends.'

'But Captain Wilkie?'

'Not sure the problem's there, quite honestly. Wilkie's tough on all the boys. Not sure he persecutes Burt in particular. Man of the world, Wilkie. Like me. Like you, I trust.'

Baxendale shook Malory's hand as they parted in the entrance hall.

'Wilkie's quarter-deck,' grinned Baxendale. 'Loves nothing better than to drill the boys here. Oh, well, bit of square-bashing does 'em no harm.'

'Thanks, Harry – Headmaster.' Another boy was passing.

'Oh well, Peter. As old Winston would say' - this in a whisper – 'keep buggering on. Only thing he and old Oscar would agree on, d'ye think? So let's see you and your good lady later on, old boy, and we'll sort out the world's problems, or, if not, we'll cleave it thricefold. "Let Rome in Tiber melt!"'

7

VAGARIES OF RESEARCH AT THE BIG HOOSE: 2012

The stranger at the bridge is unaware there of any ghosts of the Colonel and Mrs Malory, indeed she is only dimly aware (though mightily curious) about the 'events' (as they were once cryptically called) at Mauletoun back in the 1960s.

She knows that much was hushed up, or otherwise 'mashed' up, at the time.

The 'events' took place, she understands, in the year of a hot unaccustomed summer, followed by a winter of unusual climatic conditions. That summer wasn't unlike the present one – if the two, fifty years apart, couldn't be said to have anything else in common.

The stranger walks slowly toward the great door of Mauletoun, just as another lady briskly descends the steps, unlocking her car.

'Hello, can I help you?'

'Yes – are you Aileen Burlington?'

'That's me.'

'I'm Muriel Redburn. I e-mailed you … fairly recently … about my … family history, connected with

Mauletoun..'

'Oh yes – I do apologise. I'm afraid I failed to reply – it's been hectic here, getting the arts and crafts courses up and running in Wallace's Tower. I've an awful lot to catch up on. I *am* sorry, Miss … Ms … oh lord, what was your name again?'

'Redburn. Muriel Redburn.'

'Not sure if I can help. Your name's not familiar – as far as I'm aware from what little I know of Mauletoun's history, at least over the past century.'

Silence, for a tense minute or so.

Aileen Burlington looks quizzically at Muriel Redburn. 'You're from Glasgow.'

'I was,' replies the stranger. 'But most of my working life has been spent in Aberdeen. It's where I married and have a small boy. I no longer have any ties in Glasgow.'

'What's your line of work, if you don't mind me asking?'

'I'm a local studies librarian. For now. Until they sack me and replace me with a screen.'

'You like finding things out,' laughs Aileen. 'A researcher. Well, you never know, you might find something here, though we're a longish way from Aberdeen.'

Muriel smiles. 'It's a transferable skill. A nosy person in one corner can still be a nosy person in another corner.'

Aileen locks her car. 'Do come in, Ms Redburn. Can

I call you Muriel if I let you call me Aileen?' This with more laughter. 'I was going to go into Cupar, not for any particular reason, just to get out of the office for a while. But sod Cupar, sod the office, I could do with a bit of company.'

'Thanks, Aileen. I really appreciate it. If I'm really not disturbing you.'

'Least I can do, after not answering your e-mail, wretch that I am.'

They settled into a small room, to the right of the hallway.

'Nicer in here,' says Aileen. 'The hallway's so dark, gives me the creeps. Comfy armchairs there now, you can just about make them out, but they say it was once called the "quarter-deck". One of the teachers back then, he was a navy man, he had the kids on parade there ...'

Muriel gives a start. A faint memory, of something said and heard during her childhood, has suddenly surfaced.

'Captain ... Wilson, Williams ... Wilkie, was it?'

'Don't know about that. No wait – I think there was a teacher, maybe with a name like that, studied up your way – Aberdeen – for a while, but didn't stick it. He probably won't have left any trail up there. But I'll dig out our records for you, well, whatever we have, that is. An awful lot of stuff got dumped in the cellar, mice got to it. What was rescued had to be fumigated. You know all about that from your library – but of course

31

you folk look after stuff properly, you wouldn't need drastic measures.'

'Oh – you mean conservation. Yes, they'd have put it in something looking like a fridge. They'd place the affected documents over crystals – these give off a vapour, kills the spores.'

Aileen pours out tea for Muriel and herself.

'I take it you didn't get far with the web?'

'Just hints here and there, Aileen. I know, of course, that so much was suppressed or garbled at the time. I followed up whatever I could online, however tenuous it seemed. Social media, they're no use, or their equivalents in the recent past, it's all so long ago of course, and the newspapers of the past, doesn't matter whatever form you can get them in nowadays, they kept shtoom, or they distorted stuff, as I keep on saying. To be honest, my knowledge of the "events" here is very sketchy, putting it mildly. My guardian would make odd allusions, mutter strange things under his breath, but I was way too young to take it in. There is one recent development, but I don't know if it's going to prove effective – I traced the nephew of one of the teachers, God knows how, he's called Professor Gomshall and lives in Holland. He takes ages to reply to my e-mails, then sounds awful vague and windy and wordy. A real pain. I live in hope that he'll cut to the chase and give me solid leads. Claims to have "materials" as he calls them – that's good libraries jargon, though. My main source is still a paper one –

my guardian's scrapbook, but it's in a right state, damp and blotchy, much of it illegible and beyond the power of these crystals – a bit like your archive, I suppose.'

'Manky, as the locals here would say.'

Muriel smiles. 'They'd use much the same expression in Aberdeen.'

'Here's the library.' Aileen Burlington gestures to a row of archive boxes. 'Oh, these books there, they aren't actually books. Just the spines stuck on. It was to hide the door to a secret anteroom.'

'What about the anteroom?' asks Muriel. 'Anything else there?'

Aileen chuckles as she heaves forward the book-spined door. 'See! Completely fake!'

Heaps of papers and books in the anteroom. A musty smell. Forbidding to all but the most dedicated sleuth. Is Muriel Redburn such a sleuth?

She begins with the boxes in the library itself, and with a file of the school magazine from the 1940s up to the closure of the (renamed) school in 1967; in fact, she finds that Mauletoun's successor institution, Crockarkie College, had published its own and entirely distinct magazine. 'Nothing revealing in this lot', remarks Muriel to Aileen. 'Predictably enough.'

'To be honest, Muriel, I've not gone much into the stuff myself. To be frank, not interested. Another era. Different values. Eventually some of this stuff will go to dealers – the *real* books, that is! – some to charity shops, and for the rest it'll be the tip. The cowp, as the locals call it.'

'What are the plans for the house?'

'If we can raise the cash, we could have studios and workshops here – the Tower's space is limited, obviously. Maybe even a residence for artists and writers. My husband knows the stock market. Who knows? Uncertain times.'

'Can I come back on other days to look, spend more time in the anteroom?'

'You're welcome. The stuff'll be here for the foreseeable whatsit – but don't leave it too late. You'll need an overall and gloves – I'll see what's lurking in the old sewing room - it's the least obnoxious corner of what was the school.'

That anteroom. One dusty pile of papers and photographs in particular. There are documents which slither under what is on top of them, threatening to disperse the lot over the worn carpet. Other items are stuck to each other. Faces on the group photographs – Muriel is getting somewhere, if not very far – some in clear monochrome, others a black mass, or seemingly scratched out.

One of these photographs, however, appears to have been shoved absentmindedly into a large envelope, and then forgotten: it reveals a little more of Mauletoun's former fleeting population. Possibly this was one of the photographs so badly reproduced in the school magazine as to make that even more puzzling, to Muriel, than this severely damaged original.

Even so, the envelope has afforded it a limited degree of protection, and it does possess a certain clarity. A number of faces appear somewhat out of place. Slightly foreign-looking. A young woman in nurse's uniform, her grin at odds with the generally sober expressions of the others. In the row of teachers, there's a strikingly handsome if grim young man. Unlike the group photographs of other schools of the time, no names are indicated on the broken cardboard mount.

But here's a row of the smaller boys. One face appears older than the others, as if its owner was perhaps deformed, stunted in growth, or simply sadder than the others. A pear-shaped face – and (though a black-and-white photograph is difficult to read in this respect) somewhat darker than the others, even suggesting a strange colour that of course isn't there.

Burt, whispers Muriel to herself.

'Take a look in the cellar if you want,' suggests Aileen. 'Beware, though – it's haunted!'

Muriel is as rational, if less mocking than, her new friend. But she shudders.

'The daft tales,' Aileen breezes. 'Load of crap. I prefer the local folklore, to be honest. Everything about the school was so … imported, artificial …'

She laughs.

'Guess you could say the same about Simon and me. We inherited this joint from Simon's aunt, she acquired it when the school folded. Batty as a hundred caves she was, with the treasure-chests to go with them. You could say Simon also inherited her knowledge of the markets. There are no flies on an old bat: she'll eat 'em!'

They descend a stone spiral stair, Aileen brandishing a flashlight. 'Told you it was creepy down here.'

Old school furniture piled any-old-how in a corner. 'Be careful, Muriel – shift one of these and the whole sodding jing-bang lot'll come down on top of you.'

'Classroom desks!' cries Muriel. 'Look over there, at the edge of the light.'

'Good lord, never noticed them before. Not that I'm down here all that often. The boys would've scratched stuff on them – look at these ink-blots! Fountain pens, yukh. Hate the things.'

'Initials!' exclaims Muriel. 'Can you bring your light over here, Aileen?'

'Amazing to think of all this – long before we were born – '67 when the school went tits up. Its change of name helped it sod-all. '67: that was the year my mum and dad met each other – probably over a joint!'

'It was '82 when I was born,' adds Muriel. 'I never knew my parents – biological ones, that is …'

'I'm sorry.'

'Ah – can this be him?'

'Who?'

Muriel points to the scrawl on a desk-lid: W.T. She looks delighted. 'But why is he so formal? W.T. rather than B.T.?'

'I suppose they could all be a bit stiff in these days, even the kids.'

'Even him, I suppose,' muses Muriel sadly. She raises the lid: inside are pencil and chalk drawings. Among them, a bleak landscape. 'Caves on a hillside, don't you think, Aileen?'

'Sort of place for my Simon's aunt!'

'And this one … looks like a cliff, and a tangle of vegetation below … and there's a sort of pond … something in it, dark …'

'Mountain tarn maybe? Could be the boys went on expeditions to the Highlands. Or could even be somewhere in this vicinity – wouldn't know, I hate going for walks, especially around here.'

'Oh God!'

'What's up, Muriel?'

'There's what looks like a face in the pond … just a hint of it, no more … see these rubbed chalk marks, just visible through the black …'

'W.T. or B.T., he must have been quite an artist.'

Muriel sighed. 'He had a number of exhibitions. Did well in that sphere for a while. I remember him singing in his studio. Superb baritone. Nobody knew, at first, whether painting or music would eventually claim him – at that time, I don't suppose he knew himself … Well, as it turned out he became fairly famous, relatively speaking, for a while … and not too badly off. Can I hold on to these, Aileen?'

'Keep them. They're yours, rightfully.'

'That face … in the pond … it's … it's …'

'Fuck! Are you OK, Muriel?'

'Yes, yes, thanks.'

'Sure?'

'It's nothing. Over-active imagination. Look, Aileen. Thanks so much. I turned up, complete stranger.'

'Except for your unanswered e-mail,' smiles Aileen. 'By the way, I hope you get somewhere with your mysterious Dutch professor – not a total charlatan, I hope. Chancers everywhere, these days.'

'Oh him – huh! If he gets back to me again, though, he might well have the whole story. In case he doesn't – well, that's why I'm here. Yes, I just hope he'll prove reliable after all. But as for you, Aileen, you've been ever so obliging, more than I could have reasonably expected. I must head for my bus, it leaves Lettermuchill in half an hour, according to the timetable.'

'I can give you a lift to Cupar, drop you off at the station.'

'No, no, really, it's fantastic of you, Aileen, but I'd like to walk up the drive, get another view of the place from the top of the brae.'

'OK, if you're sure. It wouldn't put me out in the least, you know. But I'm thinking of the weather – it can be so changeable in these parts. Even weird, I'd say … this is an odd part of the world, eldritch they'd call it. Promise me if you get caught in the rain or anything else nasty, you'll come back here, stay for the night. You know you're more than welcome.'

Now less of a stranger perhaps, Muriel heads up the drive back to the open gates of the estate. Her bus stop is just beyond, at the triangular green which was once the focal point of the ancient clachan of Lettermuchill. In the early sixties, she reckons, there would have been a red phone box here. The red letter-box remains: no doubt there's only one daily collection now, and the little that's there will be taken to the head post office in Cupar. Back then, as now, only local mail would be placed in the box; surely, she ponders, the van would have picked up Mauletoun mail directly from the house. What missives would have passed through that entrance – boys to parents or guardians? Sad to think of it: those parents certainly all dead now, and not a few of the boys … she has known at least one of them …

About to exit the grounds of Mauletoun, she takes a last look at the North Lodge. From her browsing in the Mauletoun library file of the school magazine, she had picked up a little trivia on this. ('Browsing' – not research, as there had been so little in the file that was of interest for her purpose, and that little did not add to what she had known already.)

The North Lodge, an arts-and-crafts Gothic fantasy that would not have looked out of place in Surrey, had been occupied by a retired brigadier. In spite of the forces' presence on the school staff, the brigadier had not been a teacher, but the factor of the estate. He had not – doubtless wisely – concerned himself with the affairs of the school as such. Muriel knew his name: he had collaborated with the local church minister on a history of Lettermuchill parish. There was a brief acknowledgment of help from a Colonel Malory – just that and no more, as if the Colonel was a rival scribe to whom (at least) a nod was in order. The territorial imperative, you in your small corner, and I in mine? Something very Scottish about that, anyway: the land of petty conventicles. Muriel had consulted this pamphlet in the Cupar library and, while she found it fascinating (if dully worded) on the area's legends and lore, she turned up no clues apart from the reference to Malory, if something so brief could really be of any use. This little work from 1975 – clearly the brigadier was the last of Mauletoun's old, well, brigade – had outlined earlier tragedies of this normally unremarkable nook of rural Scotland, but was silent (understandably?) on more recent events. The triumph of blandness.

Muriel's bus isn't turning up.

At first she thinks it's late, then consults her timetable. Ah, she'd misread it before – hadn't followed the symbols – it doesn't run this day of the week, for some reason. As an information professional, she chides herself: I should have noticed that - I'm better at enlightening others than I am at enlightening myself.

Oh, well, the next one is definitely scheduled for an hour from now. I'll go for a walk. Walks are what I do. That, and bad eyesight, are what make me a non-driver. If only I could whizz about all over like that

Aileen down there, but I'm not someone who whizzes: I proceed by stealth. A bit like dear old Billy, I suppose.

So she takes the track starting from the triangle, passing the old cemetery with its population of born locals and their adoptive counterparts from Poznań and points east. The track flanks farm buildings and a paddock for horses. Having for so long been city-pent, working in the vaults of Aberdeen's local studies and relaxing mainly in the art gallery or the bookshops and cafés of Belmont Street, she enjoys swinging her arms, filling her lungs with the stink of country-pancakes, as Billy used to call the deposits of bovine sharn.

From her Ordnance Survey map of the area, she knows that on a tree-topped eminence to her far right there is a folly – a kind of throne put together from large wedge-shaped boulders: according to the local history pamphlet, it commands a superb view of the Howe of Fife and the Lomond Hills to the south – those hills 'looming like a dark whale' as the pamphlet put it in a curiously rare burst of poetry (pinched by the brigadier and the minister, perhaps, from the intriguing Colonel Malory?)

She smiles at the stuff she's remembered. Browsing? Research? Whatever it was, she's not the stranger she thought she was. These fifty years, for twenty of which she was non-existent, are after all affecting her sensibility. That's welcome. The tough kernel of the past can be cracked, surely.

A drop falls on her nose, another on her hand. It's

nothing, I'm not made of sugar, make the most of it while I'm here. I must go on, there's time to kill. Then a thunder clap. Dark whales? Rising from the deep, from subterranean waters. The sky becoming greyer, though a mild sunny autumn day had been promised. Aileen's revision of the forecast seems to have been wise; to decline a lift or a bed for the night, not so. Oh well, just keep going, thrawnly, dourly, that's the way I am. Like Billy when even he could put aside his flippancies.

The folly throne? Couldn't make it out from the track, even in the best of weather, my specs wouldn't help me. It's somewhere in that forbidding tangle, according to the map. The quarry – disused even in Billy's time, as I infer from the pamphlet – now there's a path from there through the wood to the viewpoint, not that there'd be anything to view today, even by folk with good eyesight. And there's a mist gathering …

The quarry. It's pouring. I'm soaked.

Flash of lightning.

The quarry face: the sudden luminosity lingers.

Oh no what's that no no the stone that oppressive orange features in the rock giant head of boy no no can't be staring blankly ahead it is I don't want to see him I'd rather not I'd rather not I'd rather not Pond at foot of cliff among undergrowth I don't want to look there no no I don't want to know

Muriel reaches the bus stop, panting, after the crazed rush back down the track, the stumbling, the fall in the mud, the queer mist growing thicker, the tears and the rain bitter in her mouth. Rubbing her glasses on a soaked tissue. 'Cupar' lit up on the vehicle lumbering up to Lettermuchill from the gloomy den to the west. She boards, mutters incoherently and pleadingly to the driver. *Ye're in a bad wey, hen, juist as weill ye're on ma bus, there willnae be anither the-day, there's that a haar, it's no aye as bad as this, Ah'll hae ti drive slow likes but Ah'll get ye ti Cupar hen dinnae fash.*

She won't spend this second night at the Cupar B & B. She makes her dash to the station and catches – just – the inter-city to Aberdeen. Muriel Redburn, after all, remains the stranger.

PART TWO

MASCULINITIES

1
THE DEN; CLANDESTINE ENCOUNTERS REMEMBERED

I hae kent mony a den in Fife like this
That straiggles here and there, the pads and burns
Criss-crossin contermacious-like roun hullocks
Scentit bi autumn foust; the skeleton leaves
Daunce in a souch athort the gate I've come
Or settle on the watter, and swept on,
Brak up, like aa that dees. I pause at the brig,
Seekin stillness:
Somehou a ray has filtered through
And lichts this corner,
This alane,
Juist me and this rouch parapet o logs:
While aa aroun, the reesle and the sapple
Mak their perpetual sang i the hauf-mirk.

('The Den')

It's me again – Billy Torrance.

I'm the goblin that peeps through the world's
plumage, then fair scampers between its cacophonies;

45

I'm a richt whippitie-stourie, mair than a "wee bit Fifish", though no a native Fifer; I'm the yin that's leanin on a pillar, no like Samson to bring doun the roof upon it aa (maself includit): no, I'm there, restin from my vengeful laughter, as if vengeance wasnae really what I was aboot, and it isnae.

As long as I'm left alane to make my own sights and sounds.

Imagine me – me – among that scuffle o ugly legs, the sweat and the mud, the gruntin, the slaverin – imagine me there: no, I cannae imagine it either, and I kept well clear o it. Mikie Bessop, the presidin God, whistle in mouth, never forced me inti it. I think he kind o liked me. He wrote in my report book: 'Billy never enters into the spirit of the game, and all too often stands idly on the pitch.' I liked that.

My faither didnae. 'It's time you grew up,' he said. 'That school's supposed to make a man of you. A man! Some hope. I'll have a word with that Major Bessop.' Oh no. No that. Not to Mikie. But he didnae.

The thing aboot the domestic ogre – that's faither – is that he's full o bad air, but when it futters oot, he forgets aboot it and does nothin. It's still suffocatin when he's around, and one good thing aboot Mauletoun, he's no usually around there. Nae parent is.

But he's an embarrassment, so he is, at the mercifully few 'parents' days' on the touchline, shoutin oot the so-called 'house whoop'. 'Show some team spirit!' he'll growl at me – all jowly and pink. Why, I always thought he resembled whit he selt in his shop – the pigs' heids, the sheeps' innards, the coos' bollocks (I made that ane up), all seethin and slithery. Nae wonder I've been a vegetarian since I became (mair or less) an adult.

Imagine me, though, scion o the risin scum o Balmurdie, Dunbartonshire, there in Mauletoun among the (ahem) *jeunesse dorée*, those male children of what passed for toffs in small-toun Scotland in the 'sixties. Who was the eedjit who said football was a game for gentlemen played by thugs, and rugby was a game for thugs played by gentlemen? No: rugby was a game for thugs played by a different class of thugs, that's all. No a better class – juist different.

Still, as usual, nane o them took me on, sae all things considered, I cannae claim that I suffered frae the mair aggressive forms o the philistinism practised by my Right Honourable Contemporaries. 'It's only Billy' was the attitude. I wis the court jester, you see, no sae much untouchable as untouched.

Even so, I devised all sort o strategies, wi varyin degrees o subtlety, to be put on the OFF GAMES list. 'Course I wis never included in ony team, because I wis no bloody good, and would have been no bloody good in the unlikely event o me willin it otherwise. But even us useless bauchles were duly and routinely obliged to be oot on the pitch, either 'standin idly' or engaged in the no very demandin pursuit o the wherewithal to make daisy-chains.

So at the slightest hint o a cold or a headache, I'd be doun ti the clinic. Cathy Malory usually let me aff, but Gayle – our Southern belle-in-residence, she was not so malleable. In her part o the world (I gather) even girls are supposed ti be tough: decorative, ay, but tough. She kent my pathetic tricks, like when I took the thermometer from my mouth and stuck it on the radiator when her back was turned towards the medicine cabinet. Dear auld Cathy never cottoned on to suchlike – but Gayle!

'Billy Torrance. You're a reg'lar hypochondriac. You ain't goin on the OFF GAMES list. Now git along.'

And unlike the domestic ogre, she really would have a word wi Michael Bessop aboot me. She had a lot o words wi Michael Bessop.

She's no gettin aff wi Mikie Bessop.

But she did.

The bitch.

A week or so later, I was just minding my own business – no, honestly – and takin a wee stroll through a longish declivity in the paddock. Ye had ti avoid a ditch that ran doun there, it wis awfy uneven, there wasnae a clear path, but at least ye couldnae be seen from the school to the south or anywhere else on the upper levels o the paddock itself.

I heard voices.

As I'd expected.

I peeps oot from behind a gorse-bush and there's Gayle wi Mikie-boy. They're no holdin hands – no yet – but she's gazin up at him: firm smile: ye'd think her eyes would be fair dancing. Him, he's just starin straight ahead. Blank expression. Her, she clearly goes for the strong silent types. So do I.

She's jaunty in her stride, he's there with his military exactitude. That's a turn-on for her, I'm thinkin. They're takin the better path, headin for the den and the old stones that tumble aboot Wallace's Well. They say oor national hero took refuge there while he wis on the run, and he wis wi a woman: one that didnae betray him, so it's all very romantic. The burn there runs doun ultimately under the brig that carries the main drive, at that point, towards Mauletoun. Along the burn there's woodland where the boys are allowed ti build huts and treehooses and where they get up ti God kens whit else ... Wallace's Well, though: none o us were allowed there. Too near an escape route.

There wis nae way I could follow our dear lovers to the Well, the dip levelled oot further up the brae o the paddock, and there wis nowhere I could dodge behind. Up there ye could be easily viewed from all angles, and oor pair had clearly selected the Well as a place where they could see but no be seen.

I'd nae option but to retrace my steps and head back to the school. Officially I wis supposed ti be doing my maths prep. Head of Maths was Captain Wilkie.

Guess who confronts me as I emerge from the paddock. He's been watchin from the cricket pavilion. I try to brazen it oot.

'Good afternoon, Captain Wilkie, sir.'

'Good afternoon, sir! Yes, sir! Three bags full, sir! And to what do I owe this unexpected pleasure, Sir William?'

Oh dear Gode. Wilkie in carbolic-sarcastic mode. Lesser lads than me have trembled at that.

'Billy-boy.'

Phew. I'm the only boy he addresses by his first name, apart from the elder Strang, and thon creepy prefect Henderson who's dux of maths.

Now, poor wee Burtie, he just calls him Burt, with the sharpest snap o the monosyllable, and worse.

But to Wilkie, I'm Billy-boy.

If I wasnae such a joke to them all it would be me who'd be persecuted, no Burt. He'd be inconspicuous wi his retiring ways, his 'I'd rather not'. He'd be regarded as a nonentity, no worth botherin aboot.

'Billy-boy: it's rough terrain up there,' observes Wilkie to me. 'You won't find perfect arcs and angles to practise your geometry on. Not to mention the logarithms of daisy-chains – shortage of material there, sir!

'And it's out of bounds.

'What were you doing up there, Billy-boy?'

My faither, he likes Wilkie because he's a disciplinarian and assumes that he picks on me. Mind you, I'm still wary o Wilkie. His moods can change in a millisecond. Again, if Burt wis the offender and no me, Billy-boy - poor Burtie, Wilkie would bellow at him wi such a blast that he'd be propelled as far as St Andrews, poor bugger, even beyond the sea ti Denmark – end up mebbe plunged inti the Jutland peat, dug up thoosands o years later like one o thae bog people, wi that pathetic sacrificial look on his face, his face gone even darker … or mebbe further yet, landin impaled on top o the Chinese Tower in the Tivoli Gairdens. If he wis lucky. Certainly a better fate, that, than the one that would await him …

Me, I'd hae landed in the Tivoli Gairdens aa right, but would hae taken care to land elegantly on my erse on a cushion in the marionette theatre, then I'd hae sprung up an belted oot an aria from Carl Nielsen's *Maskarade*…

But wi me, Wilkie never followed up the sarcasm wi the bellowin, as wis his wont with the others. He had his new wee dug wi him, Nelson. He wis one o Flossie's pups, and the gossip wis Nelson wis a peace-offerin from Baxendale to Wilkie efter a row over school policy. No that there wis ony tender mither-son relationship between Flossie and Nelson. They would bare their teeth at each other – as if they were surrogate aggressors, because the tension between Baxendale and Wilkie couldnae be allowed to become explicit in front o us boys. The dugs never fought, though. Flossie and Nelson were mair like Kennedy and Khrushchev, aye threatenin ti fling bombs at each ither but never gettin round ti it.

Anyway, Wilkie tells me, Billy-boy, to get back inside

and resume my prep. As punishment I got some extra algebra, but it could be worse. I never got the cane on my erse. That wis reserved for Burtie.

So I puts on my best contrite act. Wilkie knows it's just an act, and I know that he knows it's just an act, and he knows that I know that he knows it's just an act. Wilkie heads paddockward – is he tryin ti catch Gayle and Mikie *in flagrante al fresco*? – and wee Nelson scurries alang beside him. Every now and then he bends doun ti the wee dug and maks a fuss o him.

Wilkie could have made a good faither. I often thought that, the way he wis that gentle wi the wee dug. You wondered how he and Molly – that's Mrs Wilkie to you – didnae hae bairns.

It wis sad – no honestly, it wis. I felt sorry for the old brute. Molly, she wis a decent enough body, rollin alang in that briskly jovial way she had, a fag between her gold teeth. She'd greet me with a 'Hello Torrance'. Never 'Billy-boy' like her man did, always Torrance. She wis one o thae horsey types, knew that she had absolutely nothing in common wi me, but she seemed to respect that.

Ay, but the Captain. A good faither. Could have been. Probably would have been.

2

THE SOUTHERN NURSE'S PROGRESS: 1963

Gee, this dude is a tough un.

He wouldn't even take my hand – at first.

I thought there'd be some action when we cleared them branches to get to the Well. The William Wallace Well. He's their national hero, kinda George Washington and Abe Lincoln rolled into one only he was less successful against the Brits (unlike George) and got taken out (like Abe).

I had the feelin we were bein followed by li'l Billy Torrance – he sneaks around a lot. Kid's a fruit. Dunno how the other kids don't give him a hard time: back home our rednecks, junior section, if they got holda him … it don't beat thinkin about. It was a romantic trail, though, from Wallace guy's Well up to his Tower – kinda muddy and tangled, we musta been the first up there since that heavy Scottish winter – and the creek bubbled away like music you half hear when you're sleepin.

At the Well, Michael – well, at least for me he ain't Major Bessop no more – he shakes his head, says:

'Wallace. A brave man. No doubt about that. But we're one country. United we stand. Like your war?'

'Pardon me?'

'Your war – the Civil War – one country.'

I hadn't been listenin properly. Didn't know at first what the hell he was talkin about.

'Oh yeh, the Wallace guy.' I musta let my mind drift to George Wallace, not William, back in Alabama – Guv'nah George sure didn't seem to be actin like America was one country, and man, he was actin up that time, a real pain in the butt to the Kennedy brothers.

'Your Civil War', Mike repeated. 'What was it – a house divided cannot stand.'

'Yeh, Abe. I dunno, Mike. OK I call ya Mike? Seems America is still pretty divided. Abe was a brave man too. The blacks still git a raw deal. And the South, man – it's still the South! You seen *Gone with the Wind*?'

He hadn't, and this time I don't think he knew what the hell *I* was talkin about.

The summer of '63: my radiant days.

Mike started takin me out in that dinky little car of his, with its wooden frames and lookin like one of them half-timbered houses. Called a shootin-brake, dunno why. First time we went off, Cap'n Wilkie was with his wife, they smiled real benign at us. Is the guy such a monster as Cathy seems to hint? Didn't seem that way, that day. Mebbe couples recognise other couples here, seein that Mauletoun is full of folks on their own, the boys and most of the teachers. The Colonel and Cathy – I think they too kinda like me and Mikie bein together at last. But they're a quiet pair, don't say much, and have a worried look about them.

After that freaky winter, all them owls too-wooin in the trees and the wind screechin like witches on moonshine, man, it was real welcome all that sun I can tellya. Not as hot as the South, no way, but in Scotland it's like the tropics after the arctic, no kiddin.

It's rollin, fertile land, no great ups and downs for the most part. We'd stop off at villages crammed with corners where two roads would meet – you'd see folks shootin the breeze, in and out of the post office where they sell groceries as well as stamps. There'd be a little grassy rise at the townhead flanked by rows of whitewashed cottages with outside stone stairs and red roofs and them 'corbie-stepped' gables that ya see only in this part of Scotland. The bus shelters is made of wood – look like playhouses for kids, and you see kids (well, teenagers) hangin out there, puffin away, desperate to escape to the bigger cities.

From my room in Mauletoun I could see the two highest points of the county – the Lomond Hills – and I got Mike to take us there. They call 'em the Paps of Fife – paps bein the Scottish word for nipples, and Fife she is one helluva fine broad, not sexy, no, but I reckon if the Carolinas was both fellers, they'd rival each other to hit on Fife, no kiddin man. There are trails startin from either side of the cleavage – they straggle up real steep, with dry-stone walls or dykes as they call 'em, lookin real tumbledown in places, and the sheep there, they stare at you as if you was loony. Atop the West Lomond you can see both Edinburgh and Dundee –

to an American that might not seem much: you know Lookin Glass Rock where the Cherokee prayed to the Great Spirit, just above the roar of the Swannanoa Falls, and yeah, you can see five states from there – but I gotta say that here in Scotland where it's all small scale, when ya suddenly see a landscape big scale, that really gets to you in the heart, the tears run down your face: radiant, man, radiant days, summer of '63 before the world crept and crapped itself into the Great Dark ...

Was it all so long ago? Is it still that time, and I'm writin this then? I dunno what's the past, what's the present, and as for the future, don't go there.

Oh yeah – Burt. Pity about that kid ... wouldn't have had a happy life, anyways, anywheres ... Some kids didn't get a future, and I'm real sorry for it, but I ain't gonna say anythin more about that, OK?

Ah, the coast ... and there's a helluva lot of it. The sand's mixed up with coal-dust. Cathy Malory told me the menfolks in her family, they all went down the pit, as she called it. Folks don't bathe much in the sea, like we'd do back home (where the sand's, like, cleaner), but I persuaded Mike we should take our swimming gear and, man, did we run into the waves ... I took his hand, he held it, at last.

He was still backin off though, when we dried ourselves. I thought, we might never make love. No way would he have met these waves butt-naked, and I didn't think I should either, not at that stage anyways.

I didn't even think I should take the towel and dry him, or expect him to dry me. At that point, we was hungry: he for food, me for food too, and for him.

We hadn't packed anything for a picnic, as the idea was to have what they call a bar lunch.

'I know a place,' says Mike in that sudden way of his, when a few words, just a few, seem to burst outa him from nowhere. 'The Bishop Inn. Right next to the rocks. We can sit outside. Look across to Edinburgh. Arthur's Seat. The Pentlands. You'd like that.'

You bet.

So you enter the Bishop Inn by this neat porch, like a small conservatory, because it has potted plants with trailing tendrils and a wow! of a view across the estuary. Fingers of rock like they was stretched out from the skeleton of a giant witch, pointing accusingly towards the capital on its volcanic heaps. Little islands of stone, that seem to pop up from the water, and seals on 'em, lookin at ya real lazy and cheeky.

Inside, we were surrounded by dark wainscoting, and sat at chunky wooden tables and benches. The bar was ranged with all the world's bottles, 'cept o course Tennessee moonshine which you'd git back home in dubious-lookin jars with hairy fruits floatin about in mega-blindin liquor.

Words, words – man, I got more of 'em in me than Mike has in him.

I'd glance at him as he gazed out to the sea. That sharp profile. The dark eyebrows, commandin, severe.

But the vulnerability of his expression, an unlikely gentleness about the brown pupils, the curve of his lips.

He limps some – must be some wound he won't talk about – but he sure likes hikin.

He pointed to an outcrop looming just beyond the inn's garden. From there a path led up through clumps of grass and boulders to the flat summit of this tower-house not made by man. 'The Devil's Pulpit', said Mike. It was smoky in the bar so, as Mike had suggested, we took chairs at the 'sitooterie' and were served there. At last I'd found the courage to order haggis, but I'm a gutsy Southern gal so why not. Even if after, when we was atop the Devil's Pulpit, I felt like I had the Devil's Cauldron inside of me.

I thought Mike would explain something about this weird berg, but he don't give ya a tourist guide, he just shows ya places with that eloquent silence of his. I looked it up later in a local pamphlet (written by our Colonel Malory, no less): seems the bowl-shaped dent in the flat top was where they carried out human sacrifices. Think of it – ships comin up the Forth and the sailors can see this priest-dude holdin up some hobo's heart, and the blood a-gobbin into the sea. Over in Leith, the hookers would be making themselves real nice, not a pubic hair outa place, but them poor mariners would be kinda unready after just one glimpse of the rituals on that there Devil's Pulpit.

Anyways, on the further side of the rock, halfway down, you can scramble into a cave. It looks kinda small when you first see it through a tumble of that coconut-smellin gorse and nettles: you wouldn't think it would go far, just an alcove tryin too hard to be sinister, like some corny act at a Halloween party. That pamphlet I told ya about, it said you could only pass through it if you was a virgin (fancy your ole Pete Malory writin that – betcha he never showed it to Cathy!). No problem there for Mike, sure, and holy crap, I could get through it too, despite me bein pretty unqualified. Where would ya be without the power o legends?

It wound some, but Mike knew where he was goin, and there was a chink of light beckonin us outa there. So we're now at the top of a gorge, in this creepy wood, and it seems the sea is now far away. Total silence. Mike points to steps cut deeply into the stone. Now that freaks me out big-time as there don't seem to be anything human about this place. Who'd cut them steps? Spooks? When? Millions of years ago? Pretty un-American, huh?

Just by the foot of the steps, carved faintly into the side of the gorge, is a cross, with elaborate decorations weavin in and out of it. Celtic, says the pamphlet, with not much certainty (sure ain't Cherokee, I can tell ya!); it's clearer on the Pictish images – streaks of wildfire, a curly snake, a cup with a ring inside, a king's sceptre (broken), a ship doomed to sail forever … it was too dark to see all them when we was there, but if that li'l book says the whole shebang's scattered about that maze of caverns and ravines, I ain't gonna quarrel with it. I'd never wanna quarrel with dear ole Uncle Pete.

So we've arrived at a rise in the ground, a hillock with an ancient oak tree still growin outa it. Kinda weird and knotty. Suddenly Mike stops: I'm close behind and almost crash into him. He turns round: his face has gone a yellow-green – maybe the trick of that lack of light, but it didn't look healthy. No-siree. I'm a nurse, after all.

'Mike? What's wrong witya?'

'It's that face there.' He's shakin.

'What face?'

'On the corner, just where the path dips to the left.' His voice sounds distant, like he was possessed.

I couldn't make it out at first, but when you turn your head by the slightest angle, it's strange what comes into your vision. Sure enough, you could make out somethin approximatin to a face, if your imagination could be persuaded enough.

Mike grabs my arm, kinda rough like, and I holler, 'Hey man!' He ignores me: he just wants outa there. I hear him mutterin somethin real weird under his breath, like a ghost inside him was speakin. *'Asrael'*. Yeah, that was what it sounded like. 'Whaddaya sayin Mike? What does it mean?' He wouldn't tell me, it was like he wasn't aware that he said it; it was the ghost.

I know now what that word means.

We head back up the steps, through the grand ole virginity test, stumble down the Devil's rock and collapse in the Bishop's sitooterie. It's called the Bishop, by the by, because some high ecclesiastical feller stopped by here - on his way, it turned out, to be hauled from his carriage and cut down. Mike orders somethin to 'settle his stomach', one of them hangover cures (though I wonder if Mike has ever had a humdinger hangover in his life).

He's calmed down some, and explains. 'That face … reminded me of someone … in the army. One of my men. Sterling chap. Why did he have to go that way?' And jeez, Mike, Mike Bessop, he started to cry. I passed him a kleenexe.

'Gayle, Gayle.' It was the first time he called me by my name. 'We have to think of Burt. We need to protect Burt.'

Burt? Why, I'm wonderin, is he comin out with Burt, abruptly like?

'I fear for that child.'

'Mike, that kid's OK. He'll survive. Hell, girls of his age back home, they got more spirit, tomboys, climbin trees, shootin squirrels. Burt! Kid just needs to harden up. Doc Davidson's right. Bit o knockin about won't do him no harm. Ain't nothin your socialized health care can't achieve! Hell, one day he'll look around, he'll have hair on his chest, he'll become a real mean redneck.'

I laughed – to no avail. Mike stayed flinty-faced.

'Or whatever they call rednecks here.'

Then Mike just grabs my hand. Kisses it. The guy

sure is unpredictable. He says in a quiet voice, barely audible, kinda like that ghost inside of him again:

'Suffer the little children.'

It's like fallin from sandpaper on to velvet. Doc Baxendale, he comes out with all them Shakespeare quotations (so could I, as it happens, but I ain't a pointy-headed show-off). Mike, though, it's the Bible, or bits of poetry that sound like the Bible ...

I'm still thinkin, we might never make love.

But I want that sun on the estuary to stay with me, I want to keep seein a movie in my head, how we ran into the waves ... how he took my hand, there, then, for the first time ... beats the hand-kissin: though, sure, that shows class. Mike had ... class. In that summer of '63, it was great to be young and abroad, at first. The beach was dirty, the seals was lazy, but it seemed the panorama of ole Europe was there before me. Now, I guess I fear for the kids, the kids everywhere. Back then, though, it was radiant days, radiant days.

3

A NETHERLANDISH INTERLUDE: 1963

Cathy and Peter Malory took advantage of the half-term break to sail to Amsterdam. They were making the year's second visit to his nephew Neil, his Dutch wife, and their two small daughters. They had enjoyed an all-too-brief trip during the summer – it would have been longer if they had made earlier preparations. However, they had dithered so much because of their concern for Andrew Burt, and could arrange only a few days to be with their overseas relatives, in between Neil's completion of a heavy workload at the Rijksmuseum and the young family's annual camping holiday on the western Mediterranean.

The older couple needed this autumn break even more desperately than that summer one, given the increasing tensions at Mauletoun. Yet they had recalled that, almost exactly a year earlier, for those two weeks in October 1962, the wider world had experienced far greater anxieties: that helped to put the present October into some perspective. Nevertheless, they could not forget that some of the more vulnerable boys – Burt wasn't the only one – had tearfully sought reassurance from the Colonel that Mr Kennedy and Mr Khrushchev weren't about to issue the ultimate mass death sentence over Cuban missiles.

So it was more than pleasant to stroll along the Brouwersgracht on the western side of the city, the autumn leaves swirling down in a light breeze, and the boats bobbing gently on the canal. At last the Malorys, and the globe, seemed to be at peace. Peter Malory observed to his wife that peace, peace, was what younger folk needed to enjoy, not least for the sake of the generations well beyond them, such as Neil and Elly's girls who could 'switch from English to Dutch and from Dutch to English in the middle of a sentence'.

For Cathy's part, she smiled at her husband's earnest utterances, even as she sympathised with them. She was equally relaxed, feeling confident that Gayle, the American nurse, could deal with any emergencies among those boys who had no parent, relative or guardian to stay with during the break. One of those boys was Burt, and that left Cathy with a lingering uneasiness, but there had been no serious incidents over the past few weeks. Gayle had told her 'the kid'll survive'. Cathy had no reason to doubt that. A brisk practical young woman was Gayle: just what was needed. Gayle was no saint – that much had become obvious, but throughout her long working life Cathy knew only too well that saints were either unavailable or unemployable.

You had to get away from that place, you just had to. One day the current batch of boys – even including little Burt - would reach the verge of manhood and continue their education elsewhere. That would be the time for Cathy and Peter to retire and spend more time by these canals – not to mention the opportunities for them to explore more of her native county, so long associated in her mind with the hardships of the past, but with a strong folk culture which had attracted the interest of her scholarly husband. There was a life, surely, after miners' lock-outs, brothers off to Spain with the International Brigade, and – latterly - the prepubescent offspring of new money.

Neil of the Rijksmuseum bounded into the sitting room, the great boisterous galoot of him (as the Colonel would say), but he moved among family and furniture with a feline grace that was fitting for a man who daily handled precious objects. He was big-boned and his speech had become guttural, the near-native Dutch affecting his originally-native English. 'You're going native, my boy,' laughed the Colonel. 'I notice a big change in you, even since the summer. What was it Nietzsche said – a good European: that's what you've become. If only your mother could see you now.' Peter Malory sighed. He could cite Nietzsche in the company of this nephew of his, this fellow man of thought. They shared a love of history and art.

'To business, uncle!' blurted Neil Malory Gomshall, taking the older man affectionately by the arm. 'Try some of this stuff – jenever – and you'll be going native too. Then I promise you, I've got some Talisker set aside for you, wash away the foul Dutch taste.'

His wife looked up in partly-mock disapproval. The two children capered about their great-aunt Cathy, bemusing her with Dutch and English squeals of delight.

'Uncle! You fairly got that down the hatch. Jenever! And you not accustomed to it too.' The Colonel echoed his nephew's laughter, a little hesitantly at first, then he rose to a crescendo – unusual for him if not for the overwhelming Neil.

'You were needing it, uncle. Obviously. Aunt Cathy: Talisker, for uncle: recommended dose? Then I'll double it.'

Cathy waved him away. 'I'm not an expert in these medicines. Besides, I'm off duty. But take a care with my old fellow.' She smiled, if faintly.

Neil glanced at Elly: the older couple were at last relaxing.

'You were needing this break. Both of you. I can tell.'

Cathy's expression darkened as she looked away from the children. 'Ay, we've had our worries.' Neil's wife motioned to him to keep off painful topics, adding a few mutterings in Dutch.

Peter Malory stared into his glass. His laughter had subsided.

'Yes … that poor boy …'

'What's the name again – Brett?'

'Burt.' Peter took a mouthful of the whisky.

'Now, uncle. I told you, you should have brought

him with you. Company for the girls. Do the lad a power of good, be with a family, in another country. More of an education than he's getting in that – '

Mrs Gomshall gestured for her husband to say no more.

Colonel Peter Malory placed his glass on a small dark-brown table, one of those delicate pieces that add subtly to the warmth of a Dutch interior. 'Well, as I told you, my boy, we can't. If it had been up to us, we'd have brought him with us in the summer, and we'd have brought him with us now.'

'Then why didn't you?'

'Neil – please.' This, from his wife.

'I did raise it with the headmaster.' Peter rubbed his forehead.

'Oh, him. What's the name – Barragale, or something.'

'Baxendale.'

Neil snorted. 'Yes, uncle, and what did he say?'

'Said we can't be seen to show favouritism. School rules. The boys have to be collected by a parent, a relative, or a guardian. They can't be guests of Mauletoun staff.'

'Huh!' blurted Neil. 'And I daresay he had one of his Shakespeare quotes ready for you. Pretentious idiot, he seems to me.'

'Neil,' said his wife, 'that's enough.'

'Pretentious – and cruel. It's a cruel place, that Mauletoun. If you and Cathy didn't have such a military sense of duty to that so-called school, you could resign, then you'd be able to adopt the boy … Bloody Boxendell, Baxthingie or whatever he calls himself, little princeling of his domain, the jammy bugger – '

The two girls, Klara and Suzanne, looked up.

'Cruel.'

His wife, the former Elly van Gansevoort of Schuylergracht, frowned. She came from a decent, modest family of community workers who had seen close friends and neighbours one day, and missed them the next. 'You talk of cruel, Neil. *That* was cruel. It was a terrible time for all of us during the occupation – but these people … they had to wear yellow stars. My best friend Sarah – the morning I came to school, her chair, her desk, empty – '

Neil laid a hand on his wife's shoulder and whispered softly in Dutch. Then, animated as if by a suddenly uncoiled spring, he clapped his hands: 'Right! We're all going out for dinner. Slap-up place not far from here, full of little corners overlooking the canal. See the reflections in the water. What we all need, I think.'

At the Indonesian restaurant the Malorys took visible delight in the comings and goings of complete strangers in a large city. 'The *rijstafel*. You enjoyed that on your summer visit. Must remind you of the East. Trouble again down that way these days – well, Indochina I should say.'

The Colonel, engrossed in his meal, didn't look up. The children, distracted from boring adult talk by a Rijksmuseum colouring-book, looked forward to showing Cathy the results of their local patriotism: Klara was filling in the Munttoren, Suzanne the Montelbaanstoren ('Because my name is longer than Klara's, I do the tower with the longer name').

'Girls,' said Neil. 'Uncle Peter is a hero. I researched it – read it in a book – by one of his old comrades. Went back for his wounded men. Wore nothing but a loin-cloth. Saved hundreds.'

Peter Malory waved this away, as Elly and Cathy exchanged looks. 'For more of them it was too late,' said the Colonel. 'It was terrible, Burma, terrible.'

'He won't talk about it,' said Cathy in her anxiously hushed voice. 'Even to me.'

'Well,' sighed Neil, 'I'm proud of him, anyway.'

'I had a friend,' said Peter hesitantly. 'A dear friend. His brother was beheaded by the Japs.' This, in a whisper, so the children couldn't hear. 'My friend's grief – it's an awful thing, to see someone suffer like that.

'As for my men, there were many, many who were much younger than me. Some died in my arms. If that's what it's like to lose sons …'

'I'm sorry,' said Neil, reaching out for his uncle. 'Tact – not my strong point. Girls: how did you get on with your pictures? Show Auntie Cathy.'

'If you want a real hero,' said Peter, composing himself and returning Neil's affectionate gesture. 'I've a colleague at Mauletoun – '

'You told us about him last time. The navy man.'

Cathy raised her eyebrows. 'Captain Wilkie.'

'The martinet!' blurted Neil.

'As you say, the martinet.' Peter wiped his moustache with his napkin. 'No, I don't like his harshness to the boys. To Burt, especially. In fact I can't say I care much for Captain Wilkie at all.'

'Nor me either,' said Cathy with a shudder.

'But,' continued Peter, brandishing his chopsticks. 'I must respect him. Admire him. During the war he commanded a ship – it wasn't far from here – ' He gestured in a north-westerly direction, towards the North Sea. 'The Germans were waiting for them – but he and his men prevailed. The mark of Captain Wilkie's gallantry isn't his medals – he deserved those, and more – but his smashed hand. I've noticed, he always tries to keep it out of sight. Perhaps he knows the boys would ridicule it, and he'd explode, or he just doesn't want to explain it to anyone. All in all, it says a lot for the man. I'd dearly want to warm to him … '

At a look from Elly, Neil changed the subject – to the paintings of Rembrandt and *The Jewish Bride* in particular: 'The love, in that couple's faces, for each other – it's sublime. I see it every day, and it never fails to move me.'

Then, suddenly and oddly, Cathy broke her usual strong silence.

'We know a laddie like that – in the painting,' she remarked. 'I've seen that look – flitting over his face, then it goes, and you see it again, and you know what he's thinking about. He's as gallant in his way as Wilkie is in his. I'm sure of that. But he's experiencing that … tenderness, ye'd call it. More than ever now, I'd say, and at last, for that young man.'

Peter smiled at his wife. He knew she was referring to Major Michael Bessop.

Elly, aided by Cathy, put the children to bed as the men set out tobacco and whisky downstairs. Elly was minded to retire early, but her aunt-in-law opted to join the two below, explaining that 'I can keep an eye on their drinking, if not quite an ear for their blethering.'

'Please, what is blethering?'

'Oh, we find out soon enough what that is, hen.'

But she obliged Elly with the dictionary definition.

Descending (with some trepidation) the steep, narrow stairs, she was expecting to find her husband and nephew in philosophical mode. Peter had been outlining the raison d'être, if not quite the synopsis, of his thesis for the Fellowship of the Royal Scottish College of Historians: it was on Fife folklore, and 'I will never be able to complete it – there are resonances which elude me. But they'll probably not elude your aunt – she's a native, it's her heritage. I'll persist with it.' 'I told you you were a hero,' laughed Neil, who confessed that he had had similar problems with his PhD for Leiden, on Javanese artefacts in the Rijksmuseum. 'I was with it every day – still am – so it was difficult to obtain the necessary distance.' 'For me,' remarked Peter, ' it's the distance that's the problem, not geographical, for I live there, but cultural. Oh yes, I rely on Aunt Cathy for the nuances, I would say, but I have to approach her subtly. There's no problem with my interest: that's not a whit in decline. If anything, it's more than an interest with me, it's a passion. But I feel sometimes like an intruder.'

Neil shifted uneasily in a voluminous armchair.

'What a collection,' said Peter, admiring a room chock-full of antiques and plants. 'I love your flea-markets here. It's frustrating, we can't buy much, being cooped up in that flat in Mauletoun. When we retire it'll all be different – our own place at last – you, Elly, and the girls will be able to stay with us. We badly need to return your hospitality. And you can bring some Hollandiana when you come!'

'Why don't you and Cathy come and live here?'

'In Holland? No, Cathy would never leave her part of the world – her airt, as she calls it – and I need to be there for that damned dissertation of mine.'

At that point Cathy entered the room, glanced at the level of the bottle of Talisker, smiled wryly at the men.

'You told me, uncle, that along your coast I'd be reminded of Amsterdam – '

'The corbie-steps,' said Cathy.

'Yes, the crow-stepped gables,' explained Peter. 'I've done a fair bit on Fife architecture. One of the old ports, Dysart, was nicknamed "Little Holland", because of the Dutch traders there. They left their mark in stone if in nothing else.'

'So, a transplanted Dutch town then,' enthused Neil. 'Makes me think of this country's colonial spots – those frontages in Curaçao and Paramaribo, sort of Herengrachts in the tropics.'

'There you have it, Neil,' remarked Peter contemplatively. 'Similarity countered by difference. That day – I look forward to it – when we show you round our "little Holland", you won't see canals, red light districts and all, you'll know you're in a Fife coal-mining town. Not quite the tropics, but – '

Neil reached for the Talisker and held it towards his uncle. Cathy placed a hand over Peter's glass.

But Peter was, as she'd say, 'fair away with himself'. He suddenly declared: 'Resemblances between two phenomena – they're never total.' The retired colonel was resuming a much-missed feature of army life: holding forth to his men with a map and a stick. He enjoyed teaching boys, but that wasn't the same; besides, Neil was (as it were) a comrade-in-scholarly-arms as well as a nephew. 'Never total. There's always one wee bit that's not quite the same. You might see some shape, let's say you're walking in a forest, and, there's the knot on an ancient oak, and it reminds you of its like on another tree. But you know there'll be the slightest variation of one from the other. I'm speaking myself as an ancient oak who may be representative, but is certainly unique, God help me.

'It's that "wee bit" which makes the measure of resemblances between the two phenomena the more uncanny. Absolute, total resemblances wouldn't make you alert – one thing exactly like another is just plain boring.

'Now there are two dogs at Mauletoun. Flossie, that's headmaster Baxendale's old bitch, and her son Nelson, who is Wilkie's pup. The younger one has grown and is now the same size as Flossie. You can tell that they're related. But her boy has features which he doesn't share with his parent, and that's not just to do with the gender difference. It's as nature is – and of course he's inherited this and that from his father. The two dogs dislike each other. Reflects the relationship of their owners: Baxendale gave Flossie's pup to Wilkie as a kind of peace offering – the two have to work together, after all. Dislike, I said, not hate. They growl at each other – the dogs, that is – but they never attack each other. There's no violence between the dogs.'

'Not between the dogs, there's not,' said Cathy, who'd been listening after all, in order to tease her husband with the odd put-down at just the right moment.

'Nor, to be fair,' riposted Peter with a laugh, 'is there any violence between Baxendale and Wilkie. Though they might well come near it at times. But my point is, getting back to the dogs, is the mutual dislike because they're different? Or because they're similar? Do they refrain from killing each other because they have an instinct that they're mother and son? Could an expert in animal behaviour explain it to us?'

'Not our field, uncle; we must stick to Javanese

artefacts and Fife folklore. But wait – we're both historians, in our – ah! – different ways. And it's surely more than a cliché that history repeats itself. There you have patterns of similarity, surely. Doesn't that link up with – you mentioned Nietzsche earlier – the notion of "eternal recurrence", though for the life of me I could never figure out exactly what old moustachio'd Fred meant by it.'

'Against that, Neil, I'd advance bearded Charlie. I'm no Red, of course, but Karl Marx did indeed claim that history repeats itself – first time as tragedy, second time as farce. Napoleon I is eventually succeeded by Napoleon III. There you have the interplay of similarity and difference. Our comrade Khrushchev and his friends would call that dialectic. They'd call anything dialectic.'

'Aha,' pounced Neil, pointing with his cigar. 'What if it's farce first time, then tragedy thereafter? People laughed at Hitler, then – '

'In the English class,' continued the Colonel calmly, 'I was giving the boys a Robert Louis Stevenson story. A rare Mauletoun concession to Scottish literature. From "The Suicide Club" it was. There's a situation there which a character describes as a tragedy disguised as a farce.'

'Couldn't you have farce repeating itself as – well, more farce?' suggested Neil. 'Strikes me that's what's been going on with these sex scandals in Macmillan's government – I get the British papers in town. It's hilarious.'

Peter frowned. At Mauletoun, within his earshot, the boys had been taking their own delight in the tales emanating from Westminster. Well he knew that the more knowing lads would use it to pick on the innocent ones. He felt a sudden dread that there was lurking yet another dimension to the persecution of Andrew Burt.

'And it follows,' Neil offered helpfully, 'that tragedy could repeat itself as tragedy.'

Colonel Peter Malory laid down his cigar, reached for his glass which he found to be empty, and stared at the canal, pondering its reflections.

4

MATTERS PUGILISTIC, EXCREMENTAL AND SANGUINARY

Mauletoun. The belvedere: the house's view, once renowned in Baedeker and the like, of the forests and farmlands extending to the Lomond Hills – the *universe* for pent-in boys, though few would describe it as such.

It was better-known to Mauletoun's inmates as the boxing room. Here, the boys could knock out each other's teeth without the grunts and yells being audible on the floors below. It was reached by a dark spiral stair, and was presided over by Mr Mowbray, a man with a large jaw and a close-cropped pow. He motivated the lads with piping advocacy of 'the noble art of self-defence', accompanied by a narrow-eyed expression for the benefit of possible dissenters. He was known to be jealous of his reputation as the gentlest of hard men, an ex-con with a heart where his fist should be.

One afternoon Mr Mowbray wasn't there but a group of boys were. One of them managed to find the noble artist's keys, which he had carelessly left on a hook by the door of the unlocked stair, having been eager to begin the term break as soon as possible (or, as he put it to his mates in a Cupar pub, to get the fuck oot o thon Palace o Posh Pishin Perverts).

Andrew Burt was there, but not of choice. There were times, it is true, when Dr Baxendale in his kindness felt able to decree that Burt – as well as other boys lacking in the school spirit, such as Billy Torrance – could be excused the more rigorous of physical exertions (provided, that is, they were willing to act as his eyes and ears when occasion demanded). It must be emphasised that, as a professional man, Dr Baxendale was careful not to be extravagant with his largesse of soul. 'The quality of mercy is not strained', he would remark, continuing the quotation for as long as he could remember it. One had to be humane to the little beasts but there were limits.

Burt was being held down by the other boys.

'Eat this turd, Burt.'

'I'd rather not.'

'He'd rather not! He'd rather not!'

And the ample specimen of Flossie's faeces was pressed upon his teeth anyway.

'Yukh, he's disgusting.'

'Little shit-eater! His favourite meal, eh, Burt?'

Burt's trousers and underpants were removed.

'Gob on his dick, Roberts.'

A dribble descended from Roberts's lips. There was a mass rubbing between Burt's legs.

'Nothing's happening!'

'That tree'll never grow fruit.' (Kinnaird was the most poetic of the conspirators.)

'No pips!'

'Fuck, this is boring. Hey, Carey, your knife! *He can drink his own blood.'*

A gash was made in Burt's left arm and that, too, was pressed to the reluctant mouth. The time came when the consensus was 'that'll do – for now.' A pail of water, soap and paper towels were on hand to clear up the mess. 'Little wog! Woggie Burt!'

Kinnaird, creative as ever, suggested a final refinement: locking the little turdbucket up for an hour or so, then they could return, drag him out and replace 'Morlock' Mowbray's keys on the hook, and no-one in authority would be any the wiser. If any questions were asked, well, Burt was an utter wet but he knew that, on such occasions, he must answer with something better than *I'd rather not.*

5

MATTERS MEDICAL, LITERARY, AND AMATORY

OK, so I cleans up the kid; Doc Davidson gives him a shot against the infection. Kid says he fell outside, knocked against the wall of the East Wing (where the Malorys have their apartment) – but, heck, that wouldn'ta caused a wound like that. An abrasion, maybe, yeah, but … Doc Davidson and I looked at each other.

If the kid had come out with his usual crap – 'I'd rather not' – I woulda been less suspicious, though there woulda been no rational reason for bein less suspicious. I'da just thought, gimme a break, kid, you always say that.

But whatever happened, he ain't gonna squeal. Nobody does, here. It's the code, and even a little runt like Burt keeps to it. Says a lot for him, I guess, he's got some cojones after all, tho a truckload of rednecks would soon blast 'em off of him. Specially if he DID squeal. I knows I would, if anyone squealed on me.

But he didn't squeal, and, sure, I ain't gonna squeal either.

Specially as Harry Baxendale keeps lookin at me with that sly smile of his, like he wuz tryin to get information outa me without havin ta say a word. Reminds me of that rhyme we have back home –

> *Sassy gal, wherever you be,*
> *Beware of the boss's bonhomie.*

I dunno, he's a difficult guy to dislike, with his poetry and all, but more and more he seems to know what gets me real pissed. Passed by me one day, singin Yankee Doodle. Maybe he just don't know that ya don't say that to a Southerner. Maybe he does.

That's it: the guy is, like, inscrutable. You can't make up your mind if Baxendale is a creep or if it's just his way to give you a hard time.

'So Gayle my dear,' sezee, 'our Michael seems to be coming out of his shell. Not before time; I like to get to know my staff better, and friend Michael hasn't been one to, er, give much away about himself.'

He ain't the only one, thinks I.

'We need you Americans' – he drew out the four syllables of the word, accordin to what he felt was its full flavor – 'to liven us up. Jolly good, carry on!' (Parodying himself? He can do the pompous Brit, but it seems part of the act …)

But as he's opening the door to his study, he turns to me again, gives me a wink, and comes out with:

'Even so: "Lilies that fester smell far worse than weeds."'

Then he's in his study, closes the door behind him. What's the dude getting at?

Aha! Y'are caught.

(Mikie Bessop that is; and at last.)

It came about like this. Cathy and the Colonel got back from Holland and she was impressed with the prompt way I handled the Burt business. I told her all I knew – fact, I'd been totally frank with Baxy regarding THAT matter, at least – and suggested (as to Bax) that we should be even more watchful … not just in the way the older kids related to Burt, but also Burt's own behavior at its weirdest, like when he was even more furtive and evasive than usual in his manner. Strangely – as it seemed then – Baxendale seemed a bit distant when I went out of my way to raise the subject, he'd say yes, yes, and give me that hint of an enigmatic grin.

Altogether Cathy praised me for my professionalism in the way I dealt with all our patients since I started at Mauletoun. So she promoted me – Deputy Matron (yay!) with a real snazzy new uniform to go with it. She told me that Doc Davidson had agreed: with that dry kinda smile of his ('cordin to Cathy) she said the Doc had called me an 'Angel', an *Angel of Health*. (That's real neat, 'cause I'd found ole Davidson scary – he's a big man who never smiles under that humdinger of a moustache, and when he stalks thru the school, I'm tellin ya, them corridors rumble.)

I take it Baxo also had to approve of the promotion, as the big shot in the joint, tho I wonder just how enthusiastically – he ain't a medic, and has to follow the advice of Cathy and the Doc.

Cathy says she's known nurses who weren't so professional – the ones who thought their clinical care included the boys' sexual initiation – but gimme a break, these kids to me are a turn-off. When you have to finger their butts it's strictly in the line of reluctant but necessary duty. Yee-ukk.

Fact is, far from Cathy worrying about a horny nurse rampant among male adolescent hormones, I kind of figure she approves of me and Mike Bessop. She and Pete Malory like the guy. They like me. Hey, maybe it jazzes up their own relationship. Only kiddin.

Mike and I have to be discreet around everyone else at Mauletoun, and that ain't easy. Up to the encounter I'm about to relate, it'd all been kinda innocent, and of course Mike's inhibitions stopped it being anything other than kinda innocent, but you know how tongues wag. I'm even wonderin if Baxendale is recruitin the wimpier kids as spies, usin his own OFF GAMES list as a bribe – which undermines Cathy and me as keepers of the main OFF GAMES list for health reasons only. Y'know, I'm gittin more and more uneasy when Baxendale sees us together, and the same goes for them kids such as Billy Torrance (vicious little fag) and of course Burt creepin about, and ... Captain Wilkie. Hey, I got his name right at last.

For my room is in the West Wing, in the same corridor as the Wilkies' apartment ... and this night I had to shift my smuggled goods (i.e. lovely Mike) up the stair while lookin out for any sudden appearance by ole sailor-boy himself.

Along with Mike I had as contraband a couple bottles of wine. We was gonna celebrate my promotion. I wanted Mike to see me in my smart new uniform and instantly relieve me of it. Only kiddin. Actually I made myself look luscious for him – new dress, new face (so to speak), and a rose in my hair.

So, there we are on my bed, and the intimacy's developin as never before - on my side anyways: no need to steal a thermometer to figure that out. But I'm more subtle than you think: for me, the best fore-foreplay is intelligent conversation.

You understand, all the male instructors at Mauletoun, they like poetry, and they teach it. Apart from the Captain, who's a math and science man (they call the gap 'the two cultures' – if you're arty here you can't be into scientific stuff, and vice versa – weird, eh?). As he unwound, Mike started to talk about poetry and why he thinks it's good for the boys – 'Character-building. Inspires them. Can motivate them.'

As a military man, he goes for the war poets, some on 'em.

'Now, Laurence Binyon,' he's in there, likes he wanted me to take notes. 'His "For the Fallen". The headmaster reads it to the school at the Remembrance Day service. You remember, last November?'

Can't say as I did, tho I liked his unconscious rhymin. Last November was just after Cuba, and my head had been full of Kennedy and back home … and those Brit customs take a lotta gettin accustomed to …

'Now I don't weep over poetry. That's not what it's for. But there's that line' – he gulped a bit – 'it always gets to me: "Age shall not weary them, nor the years condemn".'

'It's an echo!' says I.

'I'm sorry?'

'An echo – of *Antony and Cleopatra* – when Enobarbus is gettin the hots for Cleo: "Age cannot weary her, nor custom stale / Her infinite variety". She was some gal.'

'That's very different from the Binyon.'

'You betcha. But me quotin Shakespeare! Makes me sound like ole Harry B.'

'Harry B.? Harry Belafonte? I've actually heard of him.'

'No, not Harry Belafonte, you dumbass.' (Hey woman, I thinks to myself, you is way outa line there – but it passes.)

'You mean Dr Baxendale?'

'Yup. That's the dude. But I don't wanna talk about him.'

I wanted to talk more about poetry, and test its aphrodisiac potential on our Mike. The wine sure was taking its time in that regard: Mike wasn't one for the booze – the odd beer at best on our excursions round the county – and I figured that here was another casualty of the guy's strict upbringing.

But he gets on to our American poets, and that kinda surprised me, 'cause I thought he was maybe one of them limeys who thinks we don't have any poets. OK, so Mike's into Longfellow, Bryant, Whittier, tame stuff – dunno what he'd make of that ole fruit Walt, Emily he'd probably think was just nuts, and T.S. Eliot's Prufrock? – forget it. Still, them ole warhorses like Longfellow and co.: it was a start, gal, it was a start. And I hafta say he was kinda interestin on them, tho I can't remember a damn thing he said, the wine was affectin me if not him, know what I'm sayin? More to the point, he was genuinely listenin to my own scholarly insights into our Masterpieces of Western Civ.

Then I let slip, dumbass that I was.

'I couldn't talk like this back home,' I'm there, 'Charlie, with him it's just baseball and shootin squirrels. You're so different, hon'.'

'Charlie – who's Charlie?'

'Oh … just that feller back home … assistant professor of literature, too, at WASUA, but that's the last thing he ever wants to talk about. He don't like what you guys call shop talk – leave it behind on the campus.' I shoulda bit my lip, the way I was blatherin on. 'But Mike, I'm tellin ya, this Charlie's on the way out, he just don't know it yet.'

Then Jee-zus, disaster threatens. Mike goes on to ask about the scar on my cheek: product of an even earlier relationship (I tell all this to Mike as quickly as I can), jerk I was stoopid enough to be married to then get divorced from when I was eighteen. Fuckin redneck bozo. Last I heard, he was in the pen – still there I hope.

Even as I spoke I felt I really shoulda been keepin my big goddam mouth shut. I got alarmed when Mike started to cry: that stiff upper lip routine of Brit men don't last long, believe me. As for the stiff lower down … patience, gal, patience.

Then his life story, it's tumblin outa him. Mike's daddy used to lock him in the cellar when he acted up. Even something trivial like eatin a candy bar when he shouldn'ta, li'l ole Mike got whacked on his bare ass with a cane, his mom would be screamin for his daddy to stop. But daddy, he dragged Mike to the cellar, still goin crazy with the cane, threw him into that there cellar that he (the daddy) said was haunted by an ancestor who'd been murdered there, axed thru the skull by a jealous brother.

Mike's pap was an army padre, expert on all the Old Testament punishments. Make a Southern Baptist look like an East Coast liberal. I put my arm tighter round Mike. 'I'm gonna hold you. Relax. Then you're gonna hold me.'

That calms him some, then he comes out with somethin real weird.

'Gayle' – he didn't often call me by my name – 'I'm not afraid of anything – now. I'm not afraid of anyone – now. Except – I'm afraid of myself. That's it. I have a real fear of myself.'

Yup, that sure sounded scary. At this point, I thought I heard a kid coughin outside my door, but I was imaginin all sorta things.

'Once you lose self-discipline – if you're pushed beyond a limit – and it terrifies me that I don't know what that limit is … '

'Don't worry about it, hon'. You're safe with me – hey, we're supposed to be celebratin … '

I'm a nurse, I'm also a lover – experienced on both counts – and I knows psychology. I tried laughin, and it worked, worked, I tell ya, as never before. It was like – yeah, *that's* it – it was like I'd unlocked his cellar for good and all, and he came out rampant. His kissin? Man, it was a masterclass.

Who'da thought he had it in him? Well, me, stoopid. I never lost faith. He was now a guy who was minutes away from losin his virginity.

'Handsome Mike. Sexy Mike.'

(I don't give out compliments easy – they gotta be deserved, and man, he …)

'You give me good luck. I got my promotion because of you, hon'.'

What a turn-on.

'You're my talisman.' I got that word from a book by Walter Scott – they usedta read his books by the shitload in the South, and my daddy he had 'em, gave 'em to me. (Didn't I say we had proud Scottish ancestry?)

'My talisman. My lucky charm. Oh Mike hon', you're my lucky charm.'

Afterwards, he goes into a gloom. Immediately. I thought it was post-coital, and remember, the guy had been celibate since he was a li'l babby inside of his mom. Was he worried I'd get pregnant? That mighta held him back before, but hell, I'd already told him I couldn't – problem with my tubes, and of course I'd been knocked about in my time. Whatever it was, he starts sobbin, and it gets louder, then he's hollerin – and I'm scared that ole Wilkie will hear us.

It was like when we was at the coast that time, and went off into a gorge, and he freaked out about somethin he saw in the rock.

I hold him. I'm at my most lovin, rubbin his back, the kisses are gentler, I'm lookin into his eyes, 'cos that's the way to git it outa him, whatever's hurtin him.

So he calms down some, says it's to do with his army days, few years back. He tells me about one of his men, across the water in the Northern Province when the Brits was havin trouble with a bunch of jerks over there - guys that sounded like their equivalent of pain-in-the-butt rednecks, but I dunno, I'm not into European politics, it bores the ass off of me.

Anyways, this private under his command, turns out the guy was 'lost', as he put it, durin that war. 'Lost?' Yeah – I felt Mike was holdin something back as he was tellin me this. He'd gotten close to this poor feller, who as it turns out was Scottish. When Mike was invalided out of the army – he'd been shot in the leg – he was castin about for something to do, and hit on the idea of becomin a teacher, of English, of poetry – in his friend's home country. Wanted to pay tribute to the guy's memory, create something positive out of the trauma by 'stimulating young minds'.

And then – jeez – he tells me that Burt, li'l ole Burt, resembles this private who'd gotten 'lost'.

So that was the night when I got closer to Mike than ever before – and ever after.

Again we made love – then I had to hustle him out as we both had to be up early and we couldn't have anyone seein us leavin my room and headin to the main building together. I looks out: the coast is clear: off he goes, still red about the eyes, tho I'd washed his face, smoothed him over.

An hour or so later, I'm in bed, but can't sleep. Need air. Get dressed. Take a quick walk outside. Come back, who's in the corridor but Wilkie. Snoopin, I guess.

Opens his door as I'm openin mine, looks straight at me – 'Goodnight' – this with a hint of a grunt.

As they say in ole Britland, sod 'im.

6

MATTERS MILITARY. A COMPILATION, FROM VARIOUS SOURCES

The Battle of Seraph Wood was what they called it in the ranks. Sections of the press caught hold of the phrase and used it for their own ends, until new stories of politics or sex diverted their attention. (Stories of politics AND sex would emerge a few years later.) What was forgotten by most London journalists was long remembered by all soldiers who had served in the Northern Province.

The Battle of Seraph Wood was fought during September 1958, and proved to be a turning-point in that brief if bloody campaign in the 'NP' as the territory was inevitably acronymed. A turning-point, not an end-point: it was quickly followed by atrocity and counter-atrocity, of which the full facts have never come to light. Moreover, as we all know, much worse was to come ten years later, and those 'troubles' would extend over a quarter-century. By comparison, the campaign of 1958 was indeed a 'flicker', even if that popular term amounted to a darkly ironic euphemism.

Michael Bessop was the youngest major in the British Army. A brilliant military career would have been expected of a Bessop: the family was famous, over several generations, for its gallantry. Michael had served with distinction in Suez and Cyprus, and was strongly motivated by his anger at insults to the British Empire. It was often said, however, that there was much more to young Bessop than crude gung-ho.

Michael had no brothers or sisters. At his boarding school he found it difficult, but not impossible, to make friends. Bigger boys tried to bully him, but Michael wasn't going to take that; he'd experienced enough thrashing back home, from his father. He called on considerable (if hidden) reserves of pluck, and thereby earned respect, if not quite affection, among his peers.

His loneliness at home was offset by a doting mother, who feared his father as much as she continued to love him. She would compensate for Michael's domestic sufferings by instilling gentler values, such as a love for the arts, especially poetry. Her tastes in literature were untutored and conventional – she'd have been mercilessly patronised by the intellectuals – but the boy acquired a word-hoard that would serve him well in his often difficult negotiations with life within – and without – the army.

Tramping with his men across the rough terrain of the Northern Province, he throve on both the command and the companionship of his subordinates. One private in particular attracted his affection, a diminutive Scotsman called Alastair Bell, known to be a butt of his comrades' rough ways. Michael kept a special look-out for Bell.

A more veteran and longer-term companion was a book which he always took with him. This volume had indeed been compiled for such a purpose: it was *The Knapsack: a Pocket-book of Prose and Verse*, edited by Herbert Read, and first published in 1939. The editor's preface begins: 'During the last war, as a soldier on active service, I was very conscious of the need of a book which I could carry about with me as part of my kit, and which would suit the various moods and circumstances of my unsettled existence.' Major Bessop's mother was not the only kindly influence on his childhood: *The Knapsack* had been gifted to him by a dear uncle, who had fought in the 1914-18 war. Uncle Teddy had lost many of his comrades in the trenches, and when *The Knapsack* came out he was determined to secure a copy and pass it on to his nephew 'when the time came'.

The book was flecked with blood – Michael's own – and indeed one stain partly obscured Uncle Teddy's inscription on the fly-leaf. Years later, at Mauletoun School, the calm humanity of Colonel Peter Malory reminded Michael of Teddy. Not that Michael ever inquired after the Colonel's own war experiences: he would have regarded such requests as mightily presumptuous, and would wait only for what the Colonel was prepared to divulge, and that was very little beyond what was on public record.

In the Northern Province, Michael would allow himself to engage awkwardly in small talk with his men: there were the moments of relaxation so well deserved by those working in extreme conditions, a break for rations by the side of a stream, the confidences exchanged just before settling down in their tents at night. But the Major also treasured those times when he did not feel constrained to converse; out came *The Knapsack*. He wasn't sure if those rough fellows would appreciate poetry: sure, he would tell them vaguely what the book was, but he would never recite its contents and received no requests to do so. 'Looks a bit like a Bible, sir' was the comment of one of them. Sometimes he felt that a line or two might be inspirational to the men, but instantly reverted to his notion that *The Knapsack* was for him an essentially private pleasure. That remained his stance until he taught from the book at Mauletoun, when his young charges asked about 'the blood on the book'.

The Knapsack's contents could take him beyond the easily digestible homilies which had served as 'poetry' for his mother. At one stage in the Northern Province campaign – indeed, only a couple of days before the engagement at Seraph Wood – he settled down on a tree-stump and savoured, over and over again, a stanza by Emily Brontë:

I'll walk where my own nature would be leading:
    It vexes me to choose another guide:
Where the grey flocks in ferny glens are feeding;
    Where the wild wind blows on the mountain-side.

These lines echoed for him that favourite hymn from childhood – 'All Things Bright and Beautiful' – and the allure of 'the purple-headed mountain'. Major Bessop was not particularly religious: in hymns, it was the poetry that appealed to him. Here, in the Northern Province, he could see those purple-headed mountains around him – and was aware of the dangers that could be lurking there.

Ay me and the boys like, we thocht the Major wis aa richt ken? Ah'm no sayin ye cuid get really pally wi him, ken whit Ah mean – he's the Major. Ah mean there's jokes we'd tell amang wirselves, but we didnae think he'd appreciate thaim and we'd mind the language when he wis aroond.

He spoke dead posh but he wisnae toffee-nosed. He wis in there wi us, aa the pish and the shite and the mud and the blood.

Ah'm sayin he thocht we wis a bunch o guid lads and we thocht an awfy lot o him. Ally Bell? Oh ay. Puir Ally Bell. The Major didnae get over that, ken whit Ah mean? Me and the boys wis gien Ally an awfy time, and we wis really sorry aboot that efter aathin that happened that day in Gortawhinny. We shouldnae hae treatit Ally the wey we done. But thae fuckin guerrillas ... weill they treatit him a lot worse than we done, ti pit it mildly.

Ah mean ye had ti admire the wey the Major looked efter wee Ally Bell. Nou we can see it wisnae favouritism. And it wisnae poofy or onyhin like that. It wis like the Major regardit Ally like a wee brither, ken? And he wis gonnae protect him.

Puir wee bugger, the wey Ally Bell looked, folk wis either gonnae be awfy kind ti him or awfy cruel ti him. Nae haufwey hoose, ken whit Ah mean? Thon heid he had, shaped like a muckle pear, on tap o a wee wastit body. Shouldnae hae been in the airmy in the first place – ye wondered hou he cuid pass the medical. And the colour o his skin – likes he had jaundice but somethin mair serious. Rab Simpson – whit a boy he wis, when we wis on leave at hame Ah yuised ti git fuckin mortal wi him, we wis barred frae aa the howffs wan end o the toun ti the ither, ay is that hou ye treat yer heroes in uniform, but Rab wadnae get juist fuckin mortal, he got fuckin mental, man – ay, Rab Simpson he says: at Halloween the Yanks dinnae mak their lanterns oot o neeps, they yuise pumpkins, and if Ally wis ower there they wadnae need a pumpkin, they'd yuise his heid insteid, stick a candle on tap and the wax wad rin doun his cheeks like he wis greetin … If the Major had heard hauf the things Rab said aboot Ally he'd hae went fir him, but mebbe no, the Major wis yer true professional.

Ye got a sense the Major had a temper but he kept it in. The Major wis awfy guid at no showin his darker side ti us, until …

Ah'm no sayin there wisnae times ye thocht he'd like ti knock folk doun, ony folk, us, or the Northern Province folk in the streets, Major Bessop gaun mental likes and when he'd calm doun, juist disappear on his own and no come back, that look on him like he felt he'd better let aff steam by wanderin by himsel aa ower the world … But that didnae happen when he wis wi us. He wouldnae desert us, we wouldnae desert him.

Ay, we aa thocht we knew Major Bessop, until. Ye've got ti remember that we kent him as a servin officer, no later when he worked in thon school. That mustae been anither world man.

Major Bessop and his men reached Seraph Wood by way of an open, muddy track which could have exposed them to enemy fire, but there were welcome gullies here and there, with undergrowth to clutch wherever it was slippiest. As they climbed the slope to the wood, they heard shots, then crept stealthily through thick bushes. The sun was going down: there was little time to take on the guerrillas.

However, it did not take long to rout them, though it was not easy.

Bessop and his men had to negotiate a wood that was famously labyrinthine. Legends were told of its hauntings by banshees. Skeletons had been discovered in shaded ditches – the remains, it was said, of doomed lovers. At the heart of Seraph Wood was an ancient oak, knotty with strange gargoyle shapes, growing out of a knoll where those who slept would perish overnight.

More shots were coming from there.

It was hardly the time for daft questions, but:

'Sir,' asked one squaddie, 'wot's "seraph"?'

His officer seemed to enjoy, if grimly, the break in the tension.

'Seraph,' explained Major Bessop, 'is an angel.'

'Not a word describing us, then, sir.'

Bessop chuckled, then looked round to check that all his men were safe. He cast an anxious glance in the direction of Alastair Bell.

'No, Private Gunton, not us, not even me. A seraph's the highest-ranking angel.'

'Like a general, sir?'

'Yes, Gunton, but there's a higher rank than that.'

'Wossat sir – field-marshal?'

'Yes.'

''Oo's the field-marshal then, sir?'

Bessop was beginning to get a little impatient as they neared the gnarled oak.

'The field-marshal is Asrael.'

'Asr – '

'Asrael, Gunton. The Angel of Death.'

Volleys were exchanged. None of Bessop's men went down, but the guerrillas lost four of theirs.

Then, suddenly, the full horror of Seraph Wood became clear. Blood, brains and tissue were spattered over the oak and upon the rough grass of the knoll. There was a heap of bodies. The victims were civilians – their faces had been obliterated, but their drenched clothes were not those of men in combat. Their hands had been tied behind their backs. Shaking, Bessop led the way to the atrocity, while trying to remain calm and motion his men to keep down.

It was a family of four – father, mother, boy of fifteen maybe, girl of ten. It was of course difficult to be certain of their ages. Clearly, however, the guerrillas had brought them here as a collective punishment for the father's offence – a betrayal, or simply belonging to the wrong tribe? They'd all been shot in the knees, the heart, and the head. Despite his lack of religion, Major Bessop stammered a prayer that the head wounds had come first. He knew that was unlikely.

'Bastards'. Bessop was not given to swearing, but he now gave his men the lead, as in all else. They fired spontaneously at guerrillas who could still be seen retreating through the bushes. Bessop was in no mood to chide his soldiers for not waiting for an order.

History records Seraph Wood as a victory for the British. For Bessop and his loyal band – though none of them died in the battle – it was victory at a price. The Major, as befitted his rank, had witnessed more terrible sights than his men had, recruits as they were from the labour exchange ('Better gettin shot in action than fucked aboot bi the Buroo.')

But he had never seen anything more terrible than the 'executions' at the ancient oak of Seraph Wood. Perhaps this had been a family with the potential to be happier than his own. The children – dear God, no – not the children …

Ay, the Major kind o went aff the rails efter thon – no AWOL, ye unnderstaund – faur frae that, pal. But he became … mair withdrawn, ye micht say. Juist when the ice had been brekkin atween him and us.

A lot didnae change, that's whit Ah'm tryin ti say. He

still had that wey o bein a big brither ti puir Ally Bell. We didnae bother Ally ony mair – fact, we became a bit like the Major, like we wis competin as ti wha cuid be nicest ti the wee bugger. Weill, mebbe no quite but near enough.

Thae guerrillas – bastarts, cunts.

Times we wis aff duty, we'd be confined ti barracks, it had become ower dangerous ti relax in Gortawhinny. Seraph Wood pit us in the spotlight – we wis national heroes (for a while), and the Major wis in aa the papers. The streets and pubs o Gortawhinny? We'd be sittin targets, pal.

But the Major, he's fucked oot o oor security perimeter, we're hearin he's in O'Neill's – O'Neill's! – in civvies, mind, but they're guerrilla sympathisers there fir fuck's sake, he could hae been taen oot at ony time. He's gowpin doun the hard stuff tae – him, Bessop, and we aa thocht he wis holy-joe teetotal, near maist, cept fir the odd lager.

See thon Major, he wis mair concerned fir oor safety than fir his ain.

And Ah've no mentioned that thae bombs cuid explode withoot warnin. That wis deliberate, nae phone call or onyhin, but there wis times they'd gang aff afore the guerrillas wantit thaim ti. It wis thon cheapo explosive they got frae eastern Europe – wis it Bulgarie or somewhaur like that?

And ti think that the politicians there, wan day they'd stap wantin ti blaw the shite oot o each ither, then joke and hug like they'd aye been bosom buddies … Christ, man, ye've got ti wonder.

But back ti the day when Ally, he sneaks oot o the barracks,

*likes he wis worrit aboot the Major bein oot in Gortawhinny
and he wantit ti keep an eye on his 'big brither' – reversal o
roles, ye micht say …*

*Ally wis a wiry wee bugger, I'll gie him that, and he wis
gone afore ony o us cuid grab him and bring him back. He
gien thon sentry sic a dunt wi his first … you wouldnae hae
thocht he had it in him … he wis fuckin determined, man …*

Right I'm Major Bessop I've got a gun and my men
can be here any time when I give the signal so leave
me alone you say it's your country I say it's mine and
I've as much of a right as you to sit and have my drink
here in peace

Peace you don't know the meaning of that word do
you

The barmaid gazes at me I don't want your pity
woman maybe I do

No they don't understand how I came in here
brazenly Major Michael Bessop the British hero but
I'm here but now I'm going when it suits me so let me
past I've got my gun

Back in Main Street no no keep that sight from me I
can't get it out of my head the children not the children
please God

Oh no but that barmaid think about her instead
should have spoken to her all very innocent maybe
but I need a woman to hold me what's this side street
who's this at that door a woman I need a woman to
hold me I need a woman to hold me the world is dark
and I'm lost

Come ye up, Bri'ish soldier

Leads me up a steep stair damp room but she smells nice bed by the window I've not done this before what's happening I'm inside her out too quick I'm ashamed crawl to back of room then crash into wardrobe flash boom can't see smoke fire woman on bed dead breasts blown open shattered glass taste blood down my face stumble down steep stair fall as button up trousers nightmare no no

No no not Private Bell Alastair in agony in the street   legs angled horribly away from him Alastair Ally speak to me don't go Ally Ally it's no use put him out of his misery where's gun can't find gun my hands round his neck press hard get it over with *each man kills the thing he loves* no can't do it kiss of life hopeless men come running come running my men come running always rely on them can't rely on myself

Help us lads help us is he gone is Ally gone.

Can't rely on myself frightened of nothing   but frightened of nothing but myself   Asrael

PART THREE
THE LOST

1

THE DOCHTER'S CURSE. BILLY RESUMES

Whit gars ye greet the lee-lang day,
Dochter o mine?
Whit gars ye greet the lee-lang day?
Aince ye were gleg ti daunce and play –
Yer lauchter wis sae braw!

O, I hae killed my bonny wee doo,
Mither, mither!
O, I hae killed my bonny wee doo –
It wis a puir-bit thing, that grew
White as fresh-flutherin snaw.

That wis never your bonny wee doo,
Dochter o mine!
That wis never your bonny wee doo –
Your cheeks are corp-like grey the nou,
There's murther in yer ee!

It's I mysel hae drouned a wean,
Mither, mither!
It's I mysel hae drouned a wean –
New-born, mischancit, and my ain –
Lat daith nou come fir me!

And hou will ye mend whit you hae düne,
Dochter that's mine?
Ay, hou will ye mend whit you hae düne,
Appease God's wrath fir your mortal sin,
At the coort o the Unco Guid?

I'll awa ti seek thon fabled flouer,
Mither, mither,
I'll awa ti seek thon fabled flouer
Can purge us clear, and has the pouer
Ti caum the storm i the bluid.

And whaur dae ye think ti fin this flouer,
Dochter, dochter?
Say, whaur dae ye think ti fin this flouer,
Fir the warld's wide and the wey is dour,
In whitna gairden growes this ferlie?

Ayont the east port, on the hill,
Mither, mither,
Ayont the east port, on the hill,
The dule-tree stauns, and nailed there-til,
A hempen cord waits on me early.

And whit's your send ti thon weill-favoured
lawd,
Dochter dear?
And whit's your send ti thon weill-favoured lawd
Wha bade wi us? Yez fairly jawed
And snichered throu the nicht!

This blessin frae me ti him I send,
Mither ... dear,
This blessin frae me ti him I send:
A worm in his sowel ti his life's end,
He took my love sae licht.

And whit'll ye leave yer lovin mither,
Dochter dearest?
O whit'll ye leave yer lovin mither,
Wha pettit ye like naebody ither,
Watched ower ye ilka oor?

I leave ti you this curse frae the doomed,
Mither mither!
I leave ti you this curse frae the doomed,
That ye'll no byde easy when ye're tombed,
Fir ye selt me as a hüre!

*('The Dochter's Curse', from the Czech of
Karel Jaromír Erben)*

We'd gone beyond the summer of sex to the autumn of awfulness.

'Billy Torrance,' said Cathy Malory to me wi that sly smile of hers at the corner o her mooth, 'are ye behavin yourself?'

We're two o a kind, her and me.

'I hear ye're doin well at yer lessons. The Colonel tells me.'

The auld gossip! Him, I mean, but her too of course.

'Ye're on yer way to be dux of school.'

Ay, and I'm thinkin the mither'll be proud of me if that happens, though she'll no have a clue, really, what it means. She's the kind o woman who thinks a book is a rectangular object that takes up too much space. The faither'll grunt, nae doobt, say somethin aboot me getting above myself, but that'll no stop him boastin to his mates at the Rotary. Fir him, that'd be one in the eye to Tommy Ormiston, the toun's leading baker and (ahem) pâtissier, whose son is good at aa the things I'm shite at – sport, practicality, girls (girls, bi Gode, yukh – and he's only thirteen, same as me!) – and yet he only goes to the local High. Faither'll want to rub it in when he bounces into auld Tommy in the high street. (Ye don't just bump into Tommy, ye bounce.)

Durin the summer Jessie Maclean had just been cleanin oor shop floor – aa that animal blood and tissue, but let's no go there. Faither said even Jessie, the poor auld bauchle, wis mair use in the shop than I'd ever be. He said he'd get Peggy Docherty to gie me a job in her Style & Fabrics Emporium; he used to say, 'Oor Billy, oh ay, one day he'll be an expert on women's claes – no takin them aff, but pittin them on!' (Ha ha faither, very droll.) *Being Dux be buggered*, he'd think nae doobt, *my son could be mair helpful in Peggy's Ladies' Department, being a lady himself.*

So there I am in Torrance Senior's Select Cuts and Provisions for Bespoke Banquets (he didnae call oor shop that, but he might have done) and I'm keekin at the sheets of newspaper that auld Jessie has laid on the floor. I'm curious, because the older boys at Mauletoun have been having a ball or two with the big scandal dominating the Tory Government: the minister, the call-girl, the Russian spy, the society pimp, und so weiter. Ye'd think the Berlin Wall wis goin to crash down on the whole British Establishment, the way the adults went on aboot it (or so I learned much later). At the school I'm only dimly aware what it's about – I'm only thirteen, mind – but thae hulkin brutes are goin aboot chantin the lassie's initials (why no the minister's initials when ye think aboot it?). Over and over again. If one of the mair junior teachers had heard them, he wouldnae give them a bollocking, just smile, and the boys would smile too.

But I noticed they wouldnae do it within known earshot of Captain Wilkie, or, for that matter, of Pete Malory. Or of Cathy … On the other hand, they would make a point of raising the decibel level if Gayle or Mikie were around, on their own, or thegither.

God knows what they thought. Anyway, they didnae visibly react.

Thae days, though, they would indeed react if they saw me coming round a corner. Frown, at least. Burt, happening across them in the corridor, would make them similarly uneasy. As I would soon discover, big time.

Anyway, where was I? – Oh ay, the newspapers on the floor: I see this sentence, given a line of its own, in some tabloid or other: *The tarts had no time for their employer.*

Tarts? I thought. Ye ate tarts, didn't ye? What else would ye do with tarts? And how could the *products* of a pâtisserie have a boss, be he Tommy Bounce Ormiston or the like? Surely an Ormiston-type wis the employer of his *workers* and the *producer* of his tarts as well as, nae doobt, a member o the Rotary Club.

The tarts had no time for their employer.

It just didnae make sense to a thirteen-year-auld laddie. I asked my mither what it meant, but she fobbed me aff, pretty peevishly for her, I have to say, as she wis a woman mair inclined to sentimentality than to anger. She must hae thought I wis takin the piss. But I wisnae. I genuinely didnae understand what it was aa aboot.

Though I could guess.

(Here, did I ever tell ye Doc Davidson's prescription for us boys? Always the same, whatever the ailment, real or pit-on. Headache? Take a cold shower, booms Doc Davidson. Malaria? Cold shower. Myxomatosis? Cold shower. Gonorrhoea? …)

An extreme summer had followed an extreme

winter and I wondered, come November, if we were goin to have another winter like the last. It's that Scottish thing, as that poem says aboot all pleasures havin a price: *We'll pay for it.*

But it wis sunny, that Friday late in the month. I wis doin my prep and lookin forward to the weekend: there would be a home match tomorrow, and parents could attend these and take us oot efter. My two had promised a wee jaunt to Perth for a meal in the Queen's Hotel: anything to get out of this dump for a few hours.

The prep's going rather well actually and I'm thinkin I might well become dux. I suppose I pretendit to myself that I didnae care whether I did or no – but I remember sittin in that classroom at the teacher's desk, blackboard behind me wi my Picasso knock-offs on it, and rows of (empty) seats in front, and my guid self havin a strange if petty sense of power. Bugger it: here's an interruption. Girvan, the school kleptomaniac, saunters in. Hands in pockets, the smug look on his face – the cocky, breezy, swaggerin bastard. I wonder what he's doin now, aa thae decades on? Uncrowned king of some godforsaken Scottish burg or other, nae doobt.

'Hello Torrance. Kennedy's been shot.'

At first I dinnae quite twig; me, the soi-disant next dux o school too. I'm half-thinkin: is there anyone at the school cried Kennedy? But of course it's clear what he means, this Girvan o the missin fountain-pen and the ill-gotten stamps from newly-independent

Jamaica.

'Newsflash. From Texas.'

There's a general flurryin to and fro through all the corridors of the school. Girvan and I follow our dear peers doun to the Great Hall, where we have all the assemblies – morning gym (no guid), music practice (no bad), evening prayers (yawn), Sunday services when we're no the guests o the local Calvinists. All the teachers are there and we're waitin for Baxendale to arrive and make a statement as if he's oor in-hoose Walter Cronkite. There's much buzzin aboot 'Cuba' and 'Castro' as there wis, just over a year ago, in different circumstances – 'Oswald had been to Russia' – 'Maybe it was Johnson, he wanted to be President, now he is' (a bit of variety in the analysis there) – 'Will there be a war after all, sir?' – 'Will there be more civil defence periods [classes], sir?' – 'Will we get our tuck [sweeties] tonight, sir?' -

Cathy there; she's greetin: 'That poor woman. And the bairns.' The Colonel's shakin his head in disbelief and mebbe also despair. Wilkie barks at us (at the teachers too, I'm thinkin), calls us to order; Baxendale appears in his gown, to universal hush except for Burt droppin his jotter and gettin thumped by his neighbours; auld Harry stands before us, looking solemn: *it is an American tragedy and a universal crisis. Our special thoughts at Mauletoun must be for one of its own 'family'*, by which he means *a compatriot, here among us, of the slain President.* But Gayle's naewhere to be seen: a boy next to us whispers that she's in a state of shock and is keeping to her room. (Who'll be the first to make a consolatory visit to her – Cathy? Bessop? Even Baxendale? At the thought of the first and last of these, I smile.)

Ye've got to hand it to auld Harry Baxendale: he can make a fine speech. Even goes so far as to quote American poems: 'Walk the deck my captain lies, / Fallen cold and dead' (Wilkie might have winced at that) – 'But they killed him in his kindness, / In their madness and their blindness, / And they killed him from behind.' All great stuff; most o his quotes, though, are from *Julius Caesar*. An address from Harry Baxendale withoot at least one chunk o Shakespeare would be like *Hamlet* withoot the prince, or, to be mair accurate, the prince withoot *Hamlet*.

The home match goes ahead the next day: no point in cancellin, it seems. My auld yins arrive along with other boys' auld yins. No-one for Burt, as usual. The match is a probably a welcome distraction from the big story, but my mither is her ultra-emotional self: 'Such a *young* man! The *greatest* man of our time! No-one *like* him in our *own* country since Churchill! ' And so on.

On Monday, it's the Colonel who takes us for English: he remarks that two important writers died on the same day as the President, Aldous Huxley and C.S. Lewis, but few had noticed.

So there I am, aboot a week later, almost mindin my own business, in the vicinity o Gayle's door. There are voices behind it, attemptin and failin to be hushed.

At the top o the stair, just before ye reach her door, there's an alcove with a pillar supportin an awfy tacky, pseudo-classical plaster bust. Clearly no some pagan god o silence, at least no nou, though the alcove itself is unobtrusive and a good place to crouch and, well, eavesdrop. Again.

There came through yon door the unmistakable sound of what I'd come to figure as sexual congress, though that phrase only entered my vocabulary much later. This activity was framed, as it were, by bouts o weepin, baith male and female, as if one particular emotion was sliding into a very different one. Sobs, then either party exhortin the ither to be careful, the mutual consolation leadin to renewed intimacy.

Suddenly:

'I gotta get back.'

'What are you saying?' Mike sounded angry. I thought he might hit her, and hoped he would.

'Gotta get back to my own country. I dunno what's gonna happen next, anything can happen, all them nuts around, but I really feel I gotta get back – ' and she let slip – 'see Charlie … '

'Charlie? What about me, Gayle?'

But Gayle wis yabblin on, as if she wasnae aware o what she wis sayin.

'He'll be feeling real bad, Mike. He campaigned for Kennedy back in '60, it meant so much to him. The intellectuals had to fight back, we needed smart liberal guys in the White House, that's what he said, Charlie, my husb – '

'Your husband?'

Just beyond Gayle's door, in the corridor, there's a cupboard. They keep the school's own linen there. I hear a slight shuffley noise within – a mouse, maybe, I wouldnae put it past an opportunist rodent to hang oot in Mauletoun – all that discarded food, the pervadin foustiness –

But I'm lickin my lips at the thought o it bein all out before long, Gayle bein a married woman, her heralded break-up from 'Charlie' bein a divorce, mebbe. (Would it be her first divorce, I came to wonder; thae American women, efter aa …) Onyway, it's all out now, no just to me but also to Burt, tumblin from the cupboard: clumsy eedjit must have slipped on the linen, and he's sprawled on the corridor.

Mind you, he'd a habit o hidin in cupboards or cubby-holes whenever there were bullies aroond, and this particular corridor – despite staff livin in that Wing – wasnae immune to chargin packs o seniors. Mebbe the neighbourin Captain Wilkie, though normally fierce, condoned the healthy animal spirits o thae boys that wis mair sporty than bookish.

Burt's fall occasions a frantic openin o Gayle's door. She's there in dressin goun, hair dishevelled, face tear-stained, and what a glare wee Burtie gets from her. I'm takin all this in with sly keeks from the alcove, where I'm squattin, tryin no to breathe. She doesnae see me. I don't know if Burt sees me, but that doesnae matter, as he's rushin past me, doun the stair, nae doobt into the welcomin arms o lurkin persecutors.

Poor Burt, he wis never safe anywhere, but I thought, then, that the worst wis yet to come for him, and it could happen very soon.

2

NETHERLANDISH AGAIN

Van Tasselstraat 8
Amsterdam

30 November 1963

Dear Uncle Peter,

We're all thinking of you and Aunt Cathy over there, and are looking forward to your time with us over here. It's good that poor little Bolt – sorry, Burt – will be looked after and you can feel free to leave Mauletoun for another spell in the Batavian metropolis.

And a spell it will be – wait till you experience a Dutch Kerstmis! The girls still get excited about Sinterklaas, though Klara is showing signs of the scepticism to come. Well, let them enjoy it while they can ...

They certainly enjoy all the tales you bring over from the ancient Kingdom of Fife. Just think – Aunt Cathy grew up with them, and you study them! (How's the Fellowship going by the way – I wish you could retire and make progress with it!).

Yes, I know Elly is uneasy about the grimmer legends of your part of the world – I tell her, it's surely a good thing if the kids can understand evil via works of the imagination. But best to stick to the funny stuff – tragedy disguised as farce, as you'd say, or better no tragedy at all. We're content here, very content. After what the Dutch went through, that's no bad thing surely.

Especially these days – who'd want to go and live in America?

So, let's see you over here and don't worry about Alan, no Andrew, Burt – so good that at last one of his relatives emerged to take some responsibility for him. It's certainly not the responsibility of you and Aunt Cathy, though I know you'll deny that.

If only Box or rather Baxendale could have relaxed the rules and let you bring him over. It sounds like Burt wouldn't have much in common with the girls, but they'd have had fun with him over this Dutch Christmas – teased him – nicely, I would add, as if he were a long-lost big brother come to stay with them for a while.

À bientôt,
Neil.

Mauletoun
December 13, 1963

My dear boy,

Many thanks for your letter. It's not long now and to be honest your Aunt Cathy and I will be glad of the break. As you can imagine, with an American citizen on the staff, the atmosphere here has become somewhat overwrought. The boys constantly talk about the assassination in their thoughtless way. Gayle's friendship with Michael Bessop – well, I don't know how much of a complication that is, and I can't say I care for the headmaster's insinuations whenever he and I are together and I try to bring the subject round to young Andy Burt.

Gayle, though, is a highly competent if colourful young woman: while we're away, the domestic and clinical management of the school is in good hands. Amid all the hysterical nonsense surrounding the assassination, Gayle can talk about it with a sometimes surprising calm – though for the most part the emotional tension is there, understandably I should think. She's convinced that Kennedy was the victim of right-wing Southern extremists, from Texas itself, or even her own state. I think she feels guilty about being in this country while her own is experiencing such trauma. So I'm not sure how much longer she'll be at Mauletoun, in which case Aunt Cathy would have the added responsibility of finding a replacement. It could all have implications, too, for Michael, but perhaps I shouldn't speculate on that; let me just say that we're concerned for that fine young man, whose life has been a troubled if a proud one. We've shared a lot of war poetry together, though he considers the likes of Owen and Sassoon to be unpatriotic.

You mention little Burt – indeed it would have been lovely to take him with us and I'm sure he would have been thoroughly spoiled, for once in his life, at Van Tasselstraat. I've gained the impression that this aunt of his has agreed to take him with some reluctance, and that makes your aunt and me uneasy. But we'll do our best to relax with you over Christmas! And I hope the day won't be too far distant when you can all stay with us once we've retired – whenever that can be – and have our own house with a view of the hills. We do want to stay in this area: it interests me, and it's where Cathy belongs. But you know that.

Love to you all,
Peter.

3

AT THE BURNSIDE. A LITTLE TOUCH OF HARRY IN THE NIGHT

"Folk say they're engaged,
They'll be mairrit in the year." –
"Since when?" – "It's gey lang
Hit's been expectit,
But naebody kent fir shair." –
"And whit did folk say?" – "Aa sort o things.
There's folk fair jealous, is it no aye that wey?
And wi a fortune like thon." –
"'Deed aye." – "Like they say,
Hit's aa doun ti money, is that no life?" –
"Maks ye feel auld." – "We ARE bloody auld."
"And ye say, they're gettin mairrit?"
"Och weill, we'll see." – "They're in a hurry!" –
"You're tellin me! Whan Ah wis a lassie,
Ye'd wait till ye wis thirty, at the verra least." –
"Ah dinnae ken, the wey the warld's goin …" –
"D'ye hear thon? Hit's twelve aareadies!
And Ah'm no even feenished." –
"Ah'll help ye, Bunty." – "Och, hit's no worth it,
                    Bella." –
"Naw, hit's nae bother." – "Here, whaur's ma bloody
                    soap?" –

"Hit's fell in the watter."

(*'At the Burnside', from the French of* CHARLES-FERDINAND RAMUZ, *Switzerland*)

Doctor Henry Baxendale puffs on his new pipe – fitfully, as if he were learning to smoke. The dog, Flossie, sniffs the scent of familiar tobacco, whines, curls up in her basket, attempts to sleep.

Her master awaits a rap on his study door.

Here's a knocking indeed! The primrose way to the everlasting bonfire.

'Ah - Gayle – please come in.'

Gayle looks around. First time she's been in here. Bookshelves cover all walls, from floor to ceiling. Classy. Wishes she'd known about it. Coulda borrowed some of the books, if he'd let her of course.

'My condolences, Gayle.'

'Pardon me?'

'On the recent tragic events in your country.'

'Oh, yeah.'

'It must be stressful for you.'

'Thanks.'

'Being here.'

'In your library? No way, I love old books, I … '

'I meant being here, in this country.'

'Excuse me, why? I like it here – '

Shoot. I gotta be on my guard.

'Yes – es. I'm sure you do.'

'Pardon me?'

'Like it here.' The Doctor picks up that novice pipe. It's gone out. He still puffs on it. Nothing comes out of it. Flossie snores.

He fiddles with the ball-point pens on his desk. One is leaking but he doesn't notice, and himself normally so fastidious, too. He counts the paper-clips. Spots a volume on a shelf: it's out of place. Must rectify, once all this is over.

'Ye – es. You like it here. I see – '

'See what, Doctor? Pardon me.'

Doctor Baxendale sighs. 'I wish I'd known. You could have come here before. Catalogued those volumes which "I prize above my dukedom". I'd have liked … the company.'

'Oh yeah, I getcha. I said I liked old books. Sure. Cool.'

Gayle can't quite figure it out. Ole Henry suddenly jumps up, weird kinda smile on his face, picks up from a chair a pile of books, almost a random pile, all American. He's enthusing about Whittier – 'Barbara Frietchie' - 'You'll know it, Gayle, you must know it' – Sure, Gayle knows it, it shows the Southern gallantry of Stonewall Jackson, but the poem's on the Union side, and ole Bax here is all frothy about it to this here Southern gal? Hey – he's got Sidney Lanier – that's more like it, good ole Georgia boy – and he starts reading 'The Marshes of Glynn' in his British accent! Man! Gayle tries to suppress a smile, fails, but the Doctor takes that for her appreciation of his appreciation of her appreciation of her country's culture.

The Doctor checks himself: replaces the books on the chair: seminar over. Need to be mindful of current … sensitivities.

'Do you know, Gayle, our Prime Minister, Mr Macmillan – '

'It's another guy now? The one with the weird name?'

'Yes, yes. But when Mr Macmillan was in office, he demonstrated a high regard for your late President. And obvious affection. Like an uncle, they said, toward a favourite nephew.'

Henry Baxendale gazes at Gayle with a certain light languor.

'And, do you know, Gayle, what is most interesting, they were both men of wit. I like President Kennedy's remark about Washington – a town of northern charm and southern efficiency.'

Yup dude, thinks Gayle, just blunder on. It's kinda cute in its way, though he himself ain't.

'Do you know what Mr Kennedy said to Mr Macmillan – no, never mind. I'm sure Mr Kennedy knew his Shakespeare. All the great leaders do – Winston Churchill, Abraham Lincoln I'm sure - '

Not to mention Harry Baxendale, thinks Gayle.

The Doctor stops in mid-flow, places a hand on Gayle's shoulder. She shivers, but he doesn't notice.

'Gayle.'

'Doc?'

'Lay by all nicety and prolixious blushes ... '

Silence and stillness for several minutes. Gayle stares hard: gently, at least she thinks gently, takes his hand from her shoulder, shakes it to show she's friends, like. He is her boss.

He's gone all serious. Like a Senator before a patriotic speech.

'Unpleasing to a married ear. I'll come straight to the point, Mrs Merrimon.'

Help!

'It's Dornacher, Doc. Gayle Marietta Dornacher. Miss Dornacher.'

'No, I'm afraid not, my dear. Your husband is Charles Edward Merrimon, assistant professor at the Western Alt ... Atwab ... Altawaba State University at Albemarle.'

Gayle finds herself wondering at his pronunciation of Albemarle – jeez, he almost got Altawba right –

'Which rather puts your relationship with Major Michael Bessop in a new light.'

The creep.

The slimy limey creep.

'Your marital status I discovered after some research. Inconsistencies with the documents you completed while still in America ... I won't bore you with the details ' – this with a touch of the light languor – 'But details which do not match your passport and visa.'

'Which say Dornacher. That's the name I go by, Doc.'

'That's as may be. But I have established that you

are, in the eyes of the law, a married woman.'

Doctor Baxendale stares hard at Gayle.

'So much for the research which I have personally conducted. That your relationship with Major Bessop is not, as we all had assumed, platonic, we have discovered, as a result of ... internal reports, shall we say.' He smiles, having got all that out. 'It was precisely these reports which initiated my investigations.'

Somebody snitched. Some kid.

'Who told ya?'

'Am I going to reveal that? I'd rather not.'

His smile is darker. Gayle never noticed his eyebrows before. There's hair comin outa his nose, outa his ears. Gross.

'Doc: that's hardly evidence, and it sure ain't proof. You take the testimony of a kid?'

'For all you know, it could be the testimony of several boys. Or one, as you infer – *trifles light as air*. I'm not at liberty to divulge any of that precisely.'

Hard stares exchanged. *O tiger's heart wrapp'd in a woman's hide.*

'Mrs Merrimon, I'll come straight to the point again. Mr Hamish Strang, the father of our Head Boy, is the founder and director of a very successful publishing company which publishes, er, popular newspapers of a conservative tendency. Their circulation in Scotland and northern England is unmatched. He is also a deeply religious man, *with strict views on the sanctity of marriage.* He has directed his editors to respond vigorously to the implications of *improper conduct* by a minister of Her Majesty's government. The future of the United Kingdom, and of its way of life, so admired in many parts of the world, is at stake.

'Mr Strang, as well as being a fee-paying parent, is also a generous donor to the school and in particular to its sports facilities.

'I think I make myself clear?'

'Yeah, kinda.'

'I'm sorry to have to tell you that I am obliged to inform you that we must ... part company ... '

'You're firing my butt!'

'I beg your pardon? I'm not at all acquainted with the expression "butt".'

'I'm fired, sacked, relieved of my duties, shown the door. I know some o your Brit idioms, even started usin 'em, Doc. I'm more acclimated than ya think.' Gotta let him see I'm gutsy, cool, don't stand no shit from jerks like him. (True, tho, about lingo – Mike's not the only Brit guy I ever dated: if ya pick up nothin else, you can pick up the way they speak ...)

'How very satirical of you, Mrs Merrimon. You have clearly acquired some of our regrettably current cultural practices. I commend your remarkable powers of observation on that score, I must say. And yes, despite your many admirable qualities' – he coughs a little here - 'we have no alternative but to terminate your employment at Mauletoun House.'

'I guess that kinda lays it on the line.'

'Yes, Mrs Merrimon. I suppose that … lays it on the line. We shall discuss the terms of your contract, and the notice required on our side, together with other required procedures … '

'Yeh, yeh, I guess.'

'And once again, Mrs Merrimon, please accept my commiserations on the untimely death of your national leader … a most noble gentleman, a devout Roman Catholic … we pride ourselves on our toleration of other faiths.'

'Yeh, Mauletoun, it's cool.'

Various formalities ensue.

The dog, Flossie, looks up, shakes her furry ears, and again snoozes. Mrs Gayle Marietta Dornacher Merrimon leaves the study and considers her next move.

Dr Henry Baxendale resumes his new pipe, puts a hand to his forehead, mutters, *Fry, lechery, fry!*

4

AFTERMATH OF THE 'SOUTHERN NURSE'

On the last day of term, Cathy Malory entered the school clinic to commence her hours of duty and to relieve Gayle. It would be a quiet stint – parents, relatives or guardians had already collected most of the boys – so instead of patients, Cathy expected that her time would be occupied with checking up on medical supplies.

'Morning, Gayle.'

Gayle was not there. Odd, thought Cathy, her flight was not until tomorrow. Perhaps she was packing. Still, she ought to have been there; at the least, some bairns' grown-ups might have wanted to enquire about health matters, prescriptions, allergies, anything that was not unimportant.

Maybe Gayle was back there at the shelves, checking supplies? No, not there either. Turning round, Cathy found herself facing the headmaster.

Dr Baxendale explained that Gayle had abruptly resigned from her post, had changed her flight, and by now was probably in the United States.

Cathy could not suppress an expression of suspicion.

'Well, I'll need to find a replacement, headmaster. As soon as possible, preferably, certainly for the start of the new term. I'll need to call Dr Davidson. He'll can arrange for someone temporary to cover the holiday period for the boys not going away.'

'A commendably brisk reaction, Mrs Malory, if I may say so. I hope you will not think ill of Miss Dornacher. Her leave-taking is easily explained: the death of President Kennedy has been traumatic for the young lady and her compatriots. We cannot imagine how, in her case, her distress would be compounded by her long absence from her country. Moreover, she would miss the – what do they call it? – Thanksgiving festivities, and of course with the approach of Christmas, one would suspect, uh, homesickness.'

Cathy's first thought was that any 'homesickness' on Gayle's part would have been much lessened by the company of young Michael Bessop. But – yes – Baxendale was right: only a few days ago she had heard Gayle and Michael, together, approaching the clinic; the young woman had been unable to suppress her sobbing. Kennedy's name was blurted out; Cathy heard 'America … America … I gotta get back', and Michael's replies, however muted, still had the note of despair. Cathy had opened the door of the clinic and allowed Gayle to fall into her arms, directing Michael to the sink for some means of revival.

And now this news from Baxendale. Cathy retained her wariness, but she thought: Well, this is it. Gayle's gone. She'll no be back. Hou is young Mikie goin ti tak this? The puir laddie.

'Headmaster,' said Cathy, mindful of her professional composure. 'I was very fond of the lassie … Miss Dornacher. She was good with the boys. Not what you'd call warm, but ay, efficient, no-nonsense – that's it, no-nonsense. We all of us have to deal with nonsense from the boys, and deal with it in our own way – '

'Admirably put,' said Dr Baxendale, ' if I may say so, Mrs Malory.'

'She's gone,' announced Cathy Malory to her husband.

He threw down his paper, rose stiffly from his armchair.

'The poor boy.'

'Ay … Michael.'

'I meant Burt – the way she dealt with his injuries, and yes, too, her intolerance of the bullies - she knew how to freeze them out – but yes, yes, Mike too. If only *he* could come to Amsterdam with us, but it's too late to arrange that – '

'Dinna be daft, Pete. What would Michael dae in Amsterdam?'

'Yes, yes, fish out of water, I suppose. Nothing in common with our Neil. Awkward with the children, I shouldn't wonder. You're right, Cathy. As always.'

Michael, thought Cathy, *the poor boy indeed. If Baxendale wasnae goin ti have thon lassie Gayle, naebody was.*

'Very strange,' she said.

'What was that, Cathy?'

'Och, just the way thon time … oh when that couple, thae parents, handed me a set of bathroom towels, for the "engaged couple".'

'Oh yes, there was that.'

'I had to explain to them that Mr Bessop and Miss Dornacher were not in fact engaged, the two were "just good friends" (the things I have to say to folk sometimes …) that their bairn had, uh! misinterpreted the situation.'

'Yes, yes, Cathy, these boys, they can be so naïve.'

Cathy raised an eyebrow. 'Well, I'm no sae sure, Pete. That laddie o theirs, I know him, sort of boy who wouldnae care for the possible consequences of his mischief … '

'Ah yes, I think I know who you mean, Cathy.'

'Do ye? Och weill. It's over now, whatever it was between our "engaged couple".'

'Poor Mike.'

Peter took up his paper again as Cathy put on the kettle.

'Not poor Burt though,' he found himself saying.

'Wee Andy … ay, he'll have been collected by now.'

'Yes, that's strange, of course I'd remembered that, but I thought he'd come and say goodbye. I was sorting out the history books upstairs, maybe he didn't want to disturb me – '

'Polite wee boy, Andy.'

'Did he not say goodbye to you?'

'No – though he'd know where to find me, I was in the clinic, he's been there often enough … '

'Some reason no doubt, my dear. Not wanting to disturb. Thoughtful little fellow. Still, it would have been nice to know when that aunt was picking him up. I asked the headmaster but he wasn't sure – you'd think he'd make a point of finding out. Burt being a special case.'

Cathy served the tea, with caramel wafers – 'Your favourite, Pete.'

'Yes, yes, my indulgence. Well, we're almost packed. This time we can relax with Neil and the family as never before. Damn, my papers in a pile here – where are the tickets?'

'Nae bother, Pete. I put them in my handbag. Relax. Tomorrow we'll be in Amsterdam. It'll be a fine Christmas – Kerstmis. Away from this madhouse for a few weeks.' She looked questioningly at her husband.

'I'm fine, m'dear. I'm so relieved that the aunt came forth. And assured. Dr Baxendale says he was impressed by the lady, told me that Andrew Burt would be well provided for.'

There was a knock on the door. The Christmas spirit indeed: it was Captain Wilkie, accompanied by his wife. The Captain's face bore no trace of sourness. He informed the Malorys that, at long last, in their early forties, he and Molly were expecting their first child.

'The dog's nose will be put out joint,' laughed Mrs Wilkie.

The Malorys exchanged looks of a wan benevolence. The Colonel extended his hand to that of the Captain and shook it vigorously. The ladies embraced. The couples wished each other all happiness for Christmas and in 1964: it looked to be a far better year than the one which was about to pass.

Except, thought Cathy ruefully, *for Gayle and Michael. At least for Michael.*

5

QUEST AND QUARRY

Then Lamkin's taen a sherp knife,
That hung doun bi 's gaire,
And he has gien the bonny babe
A deep wound and a sair.

Then Lamkin he rocked,
And the fause nourice sang,
Till frae ilka bore o the cradle
The reid blood oot sprang.

('Lamkin, or Lord Wearie's
Castle', a traditional Fife ballad)

The *haar*: it is that cold mist unique to the east coast of Scotland, and in particular to Fife. The *haar*: a long-vowelled word for a long-lasting condition, unpopular with sea-goers and landsfolk alike.

In the mid-to-late winter of 1963-64, the one which was not supposed to be as harsh as that of the year before, the *haar* thickened into such a fog as had never been equalled in living memory. There were those foolish enough to go hiking beyond the towns in search of ancient monuments: approaching a ruined castle of their choice, their destination would come upon them quite bone-searingly, as they would not have expected a monster so misshapen and predatory. The broken bars on gaping windows were as teeth to crush the trespasser. Turrets and stairwells rose like mocking knights intent on punishing the presumption of amateur historians.

Even those seasoned savants who monologued to each other in the pubs of royal Falkland, undertaking their reluctant departure from the alco-erotic delights of the bar, even they crept warily along the village pavement in case the Palace of the Stuarts leapt out at them from the phlegm-grey nowhere.

The *haar* is, above all, *dreich*.

No English word will do: *dreich* in itself is compact of all unwelcome words beginning with *dr*. Dreary, drizzly ... even then you soon run out of English words and only other Scots words will serve for anything approaching a definition ... *drabbly*, *drabblichy* even, *droukit*, *drowie*, *drumlie* .... Well, just *dreich*, that says it all. In its own grim perversity, *haar* has to be different and begin not with the usual *dr* but with a *h*, followed by that vowel that threatens to extend itself well into the spring and summer, and probably will.

Mauletoun's parents and staff, both, experienced an unprecedented anxiety at the beginning of the new term. Would all the boys make it to the school in time for the first classes? Mauletoun's fees were steep and no-one wanted their son to be skimped of education.

The last car-lights loomed up the brae towards the lodge, the last child having been dropped off, his parents intent on heading home before the impenetrability became all-conquering. Cathy Malory had directed Mrs Makarowski to stock up the freezers to full capacity, as no-one knew when deliveries could safely resume.

The last child was dropped off – it had been expected that he would be Andrew Burt, as everyone else had been accounted for.

The last child dropped off was not Andrew Burt.

Cathy Malory overheard one boy squeak croakingly to another: 'Burtie! He's still to come! He'll be late for his own funeral!'

The second boy, famous for mimickry, added: 'Turn up for his funeral! He'd rather not!'

Cathy shivered.

At first it was thought that Burt's aunt would be keeping him at home until the fog 'dissipated' – but when would that happen? If such was the case, moreover, why hadn't the aunt phoned?

Cathy put this to her husband and, of necessity, to the headmaster.

'I'm sorry, Mrs Malory,' said Dr Baxendale, 'that you should come back to such a trouble, after a well-deserved séjour in old Batavia. Vex not your spirit, a simple phone-call will explain all.'

'Mrs Latto?'

'Yes?'

'Good evening, Mrs Latto. It's Cathy Malory here, from Mauletoun.'

'Yes, what's the problem?'

'Mrs Latto?'

'I'm still here.'

'Your nephew hasn't appeared. We thought you might have had difficulty in return – '

'He's not here.'

'What? Excuse me, I don't understand.'

'He never came.'

Mrs Latto, Cathy thought much later, must have been one of these women whose 'phone' manner would be no different in a face-to-face encounter.

For the present, Cathy instinctively controlled her feelings of alarm with a sense that practicality must prevail, wherever it might take her.

'But why didn't you tell us, Mrs Latto? A quick call, there's always someone here to pick up the phone. Have you any idea where Andrew might be?'

'Excuse me, Mrs Mal … '

'Malory.'

'Mrs Malory, I saw no need to phone you. Someone at the school phoned me.'

'Someone at the school phoned you?'

'That's what I said. I assumed it was someone at the school, who else would it be?'

Cathy swayed on her feet.

'Whose voice was it, Mrs Latto?'

'Hard to say. They didn't give a name.'

'Didn't you ask?'

'Look, Mrs Malory, it's not my kid. I've had enough of my own in my time – '

'Was it his mother? His father? Making alternative arrangements for him?'

'Difficult to say if it was a man's voice or a woman's. Or the accent. Not even sure it was an adult's voice … the line was very bad, crackly.'

'So it might have been his parents, trying to phone you from Ceylon.' Cathy knew that the parents were separated, and that the father or mother would ring individually, if at all. 'Or someone there speaking on their behalf – a native employee?'

'Possibly. A rare occurrence if it was. I'm not in touch with my sister much. Turns her nose up at our side of the family. Her type, they get a bit of money and – '

'But Mrs Latto, how had they arranged with you in the first place to look after Andrew during the holiday?'

'It was nothing to do with them. It was my husband, he took pity on the kid, so we offered to take him.'

'Mrs Latto, I have to ask you again - couldn't you have asked who was phoning?'

'No time. It was all so quick.'

Cathy felt this was getting nowhere – obviously: Mrs Latto was in no hurry to reveal the substance of the phone call - something, surely, must have been communicated, even through a bad line. So, the initial shock and panic behind her, Cathy regained her professional cool, her ability to act promptly in a crisis. Nothing in her training, she reflected later, had prepared her for anything like this, and a sense of failure and guilt would never leave her after that day.

The unknown voice, whether or not it belonged to a member of the Mauletoun staff, had managed to communicate to Mrs Latto that Andrew would, after all, be staying at the school during the vacation: the parents had changed their mind and did not wish to 'burden' (Mrs Latto had caught that word clearly enough) his aunt with his presence. Andrew would be 'well provided for' and would enjoy his Christmas. Then that was it. The line, said Mrs Latto curtly, had gone dead.

This is within the school, Cathy concluded, *it's got nothing to do with Ceylon.* She lost no more time. As soon as she put the phone down on Mrs Latto, she called the police.

Having completed an inspection of the school's heating system, as the fog was accompanied by a cold spell rivalling the previous year at its worst, Peter entered the apartment. Cathy told him of the emergency. Her husband was accustomed to her laconic ways; rationally, he would never have mistaken them for callousness. Nevertheless, on this occasion, her manner of breaking the news sounded as brutal as the news itself.

'I'll inform Baxendale – and Wilkie,' blurted the Colonel, once he had regained his composure; his customary regard for titles had lapsed – they were plain Baxendale and Wilkie.

'I'll break it gently to young Michael,' he added,

shaking. If only Cathy had broken it gently to himself. But the poor young fellow, their closest colleague, would be especially vulnerable at this time, after the sudden loss of Gayle. Vulnerable? Fragile, more like. Michael had been so attentive to little Andrew's welfare, as far as was permissible according to the school's regulations on the avoidance of favouritism. However intense the relationship with Gayle, she could never have distracted him from his care for the boy.

Just now, these thoughts came to him fitfully and below the level of full consciousness. It was only in his later and final years that Peter added the Mauletoun period, at its worst, to his constant sense that the challenges of peace could at times match those of war.

The *haar* got worse.

Driving became difficult for the emergency services, and impossible for everyone else. Stockpiles of food, fuel and medicines were well under control – those in positions of responsibility, public or domestic, had for the most part 'seen it coming', but nobody could predict when light and clarity would be restored to nature.

The police search for Andrew Burt was of course seriously hindered. The most powerful electric torches and searchlights were inadequate to the task; Cathy produced the child's bedding and those clothes recently worn by him – pyjamas, dressing gown – but the best-trained sniffer dogs remained defeated. The school buildings having been thoroughly searched, as well as the grounds (as far as was possible), the task grew increasingly demanding as officers fanned out to the surrounding countryside.

It made sense for the police to reside in the school; in such a large house, rooms could be found to accommodate everyone. The officers found Cathy and Peter to be more helpful than any other adult. They obtained whatever sense they could out of the boys, but initially that wasn't much; the sterling exception was the head boy, Donald Strang, a young man who would clearly go far. He was in a good position to tell the police the extent of Burt's ordeals, or at least those of which he had been aware: he gave the officers the names of the worst bullies, to whom further questions could be addressed. Very useful indeed.

Billy Torrance, like everyone else, was plied for information. At first reluctant to be a 'clype', he was warned by the officers that he must tell them what he knew. He confirmed the names of the bullies, and was relieved not to be asked about anything else. The police were unimpressed by his 'jessie' ways, but ruled him out as a reliable source of knowledge concerning Burt's disappearance. (Of course, the family and its Ceylonese connections still had to be investigated, 'internal' though the case might be, but the officers' colleagues in Mrs Latto's home town were unable to get any more out of her than had Cathy; the aunt's ignorance seemed genuine if unlovely, and she was eliminated from further enquiries. Contacting the parents in Ceylon by phone was of course extremely demanding: the mother was hysterical, the father impossibly distant, emotionally as well as geographically. The Ceylonese police had other priorities.)

As for the man who was supposed to be in charge at Mauletoun, Dr Henry Baxendale, the uniformed consensus was that he was a bit of a nutter, a possible but not a probable suspect, though worth keeping an eye on. Captain Wilkie attracted the police's respect from the beginning. He told them that, relative to other members of staff, he hadn't had much to do with Burt – or Andrew as he now called him – as he took special responsibility for those boys who showed promise in naval and scientific studies; Burt – Andrew – didn't come into that category. The Captain was candid about the discipline to which he had subjected the boy – 'firm but fair' – and one day young Andrew would be thankful for his efforts to toughen him up for a tough world.

'I hope,' said one of the officers, 'that he will have the opportunity to thank you in person, sir.'

'Indeed,' replied Wilkie.

The officer noted a slight tremor of the Captain's lower lip, though the rest of the face looked frank and resolute.

'Thank you, Captain Wilkie. I've no further questions for the present. I understand that you need to attend to your wife.'

'Yes.' Mrs Wilkie's pregnancy was proving to be a difficult one; Cathy Malory and Dr Davidson (himself now unusually resident at Mauletoun) were continuing to do their best for her at a time of general turmoil throughout the school.

The police were getting nowhere with Michael Bessop. He could not answer their questions coherently. Cathy asked them if it would help if she and Dr Davidson could be with them during the questioning of the young man.

At last, there emerged a clue – cryptic enough - from the ramblings of the young man.

Rock ... face ...

Bessop repeated these words over and over again. Peter, told of this, joined the group attending to him. Suddenly it occurred to Peter: between them, he and Michael would take the boys for their Sunday walks, and there were certain features of that austere landscape ...

Rock ... face ... quarry.

But how to get there, let alone search? The *haar* was thicker than ever.

The questioning of Bessop continued, as much as it could, but the man was in a terrible state.

It was many weeks before the search could resume. The quarry covered a wide area. Brambles and nettles would need to be cleared. It would be muddy and the long rain would have created pools.

Eventually the day came when Michael Bessop could

be led from the school, up the brae to the hamlet of Lettermuchill, and along the farm track to the quarry. The *haar* had eased; it had not altogether dispersed.

As they approached the long-excavated area, Bessop screamed in terror.

Rock … face …

And he pointed tremblingly to a corner of the sandstone cliff. It did indeed resemble a face if you saw it from a particular angle: move your head a little, the likeness would vanish. The police remained puzzled.

The thick vegetation was being painstakingly removed at the foot of the quarry. Two (and sometimes more) officers had to restrain the hysterical Bessop.

Rock … face … Bell … Burt … Alastair … Andrew … Ally … Andy …

'Sir!'

The officer who called his superior had discovered a deep pool behind what had been an especially recalcitrant tangle of thorns. The dogs were becoming increasingly excited.

The pool was slowly and patiently drained. The men were clad in thick rubber and were covered in mud and slime. At last there appeared what looked like the body of a child, decomposed, sodden, unrecognisable.

The school's visiting dentist, Mr Thomson of Auchtermyre, confirmed from his records that the corpse was that of Andrew Burt. Michael Bessop was arrested, charged with murder, and taken into custody.

His rooms in Mauletoun were of course thoroughly

searched. 'Here, sir' – an officer had found a book, *The Knapsack*, stained with blood. It could be used in evidence. Whatever forensic tests were available at that time would be applied to the volume and to the accused's other effects.

During the interrogation – such as it was – the words *Each man kills the thing he loves* were uttered frequently by the accused. His relationship with Gayle Marietta Merrimon, also known as Dornacher, had been factored into the enquiries. *Had he disposed of her as well?* – No: she was back in the States. – Should we seek her extradition? – She couldn't be traced, there was only a record that she had re-entered her own country. Her husband in the state of Altawba had no idea where she was: maybe taken up with another man. – What were the police over there saying about it? – Nothing much. A lot of shit happens in the States, man. – Our President got killed, the country's fucked up, who's gonna freak out over some broad? – Yeh, trailer trash. Anyway, you got the guy, didncha? Let him fry.

That American cop's advice was echoed – in her fashion – by Mrs Euphemia Burt, the distraught mother of the murdered boy. 'Hanging's too good for Bessop. Major? I'll Major him. He should be court-martialled and shot. Why should the hard-working taxpayers of the UK have the expense of trying such scum?' Her husband, to whom she was currently if briefly reconciled, attempted to comfort her on their

Colombo verandah, but he was shooed away. 'My beautiful boy!' sobbed Mrs Burt, and buried her face in the tresses of Rory, her favourite Afghan hound.

At the time, Britain was in the throes of a debate on capital punishment, and in Parliament the abolitionists were gaining ground. Recent executions in Aberdeen and Manchester would prove to be the last. The tabloids were divided: some clamoured for a guilty verdict followed swiftly by the ultimate penalty; others feared to issue premature pronouncements on a war hero who might not, after all, have slaughtered an innocent child. It wasn't, surely, an open and shut case.

The trial was a confused and often frenzied affair, a *cause célèbre*, if also (oddly and often) *sotto voce*.

Counsel for Bessop's defence argued that, in view of his long endurance of severe bullying, the boy might have committed suicide. Nonsense, said that prosecution, how would that explain the cracked skull? Defence: he could have fallen into the quarry and smashed his head on rocks below. Prosecution: that is so far-fetched as to be laughable. (Nobody laughed.) Defence: a boy or boys could have killed him – the ultimate form of bullying. Prosecution: the boys had been questioned, they are not as tough as they think they are, they would have broken down before the stare of a determined investigator. Defence: were we even sure the body was that of Burt? The Auchtermyre dentist, Mr Archibald Thomson, was a known soak, whose patients dreaded his shaking fingers – he could have muddled up his dental records during one of his 'lapses', and we know that another of his young patients, a local boy of Burt's age, had gone missing around the same time and the search for him had also been impeded by the unusual weather conditions. Perhaps, then, Andrew Burt was still alive somewhere. Prosecution: come, come, my learned friend is getting desperate.

Under increasingly intense interrogation, Bessop had confessed to the murder, then retracted. The accused's performance in the witness box had not favourably impressed the jury – he was aggressive, foul-mouthed (as was unfamiliar to those who knew him) and he appeared to be drunk. For the defence, Dr Davidson attempted to explain such behaviour as the result of the medication he had prescribed for the patient ('the murderer!' someone shouted in court, then was ushered out). This man, argued the doctor, needed not punishment but treatment.

It was becoming clear, though, that all was not going well for the young man. Could a lesser plea of manslaughter be pursued?

Colonel Peter Malory and Captain Norman Wilkie were called as character witnesses for the defence. Their testimonies were almost identical: as men who had experienced combat, they understood what appalling circumstances could drive brave but sensitive men to criminal activities. The court must take account of

the horrors of Seraph Wood and Gortawhinny: Mr –
Major – Michael Bessop had displayed exceptional
gallantry in the Northern Province but had paid a
terrible personal price. The nation should honour such
men, should protect them from themselves, not hound
them to the gallows.

The Colonel and the Captain went on to cite –
both with marked reluctance - details from their
own individual service, respectively in the Army
out East, and in the Navy during the North Sea and
Mediterranean campaigns.

The High Court judge, himself a distinguished
former officer, was moved to refer to the signal service
performed by members of the Bessop family over
several generations, and including the accused.

Major Michael Bessop was committed to the State
Hospital at Dunarty. He might never be discharged.

For Mauletoun School, rumour, fantasy and scandal
fed each other. Dr Henry Baxendale, having emptied
a bottle of Chivas Regal ('Cup us, till the world go
round'), blurted out his witness of real or imagined
sexual encounters between Bessop, himself, other
male staff, and 'that foul American strumpet'. Parents
began to mutter that 'she' must also have debauched
the boys – the things these kids were saying about
outgoing Ministers of the Crown! – and an outraged
Mr Hamish Strang, father of the Head Boy, withdrew
his sponsorship of the school's present and projected
facilities.

The school governors eventually got round to sacking Henry Baxendale, ordering the temporary suspension of the school, then resurrecting it as Crockarkie College. Many, but not all, of Mauletoun's staff and boys sought their futures elsewhere. That the Malorys and the Wilkies were staying on, at least for a while, reassured a good number of parents (especially those who feared much higher fees at any rival institution). Unfortunately, Crockarkie College, designed as a compromise between the censoriously religious of its new staff intake, and the more liberal, cultivated linguists and intellectuals of their equally new colleagues, proved a failure. Calvinism and cosmopolitanism - not a wise blend. Despite their qualities and the respect they had so recently attracted, the Malorys and the Wilkies could not keep peace between the rival factions. Parents who were partisan to either side, as well as the non-aligned, began to withdraw their offspring. Captain Wilkie was the last survivor of the *ancien régime*, and he got out shortly before Crockarkie's closure in 1967.

6

BILLY'S VALHALLA VALEDICTION

'Twas ever thus: ay, but there are different kinds o thusness.

Here, then, beginneth the last testament of Billy Torrance, superfluous man. As the twenty-first century reaches and retches oot before me, I have only *fragments to shore* ... Och, I'm as bad as auld Henry Baxendale, all thir scraps o quotations, sae difficult to bundle up into a whole, but there's nae hope o wholeness.

The dear parents, on Mauletoun's suspension, despatched me (wi some reluctance) to a like institution, thence to what is quaintly called a 'public' school. There I experienced a number o unsatisfactory fumbles, but for the maist part I blocked oot all else by means o art, music, literature and – study. I'm no endowed overmuch with the Proddy ethic, but I excelled effortlessly in what I love, became dux, and my housemaster advised me to apply to Cambridge to acquire, as he pit it, 'some Southern sophistication'. (What do ye think o that, Gayle, wherever ye are?)

Instead, I applied to Glasgow, wis accepted, and discovered mair o the arts than I'd ever thought existed. The city gave me opera, Lieder, galleries, architecture, and design (I was inti Charles Rennie Mackintosh in the '70s, before he became fashionable); the university gave me the library stack room, where I browsed in retreat from the official booklists – I could stand there, on that metal floor, absorbed in a book aboot James Ensor's paintings and find mysel swayin as my legs numbed. There were the classes, o course, tedious for the maist part, but at least they were signposts towards a range o European literature, including Scottish: Peter Malory had started us aff wi that last, but he could hardly gang far wi it, Mauletoun bein as it was.

Ah yes, Scotland. And no just Scotland. Today.

All thae solemn pronouncements aboot football; the Burns Supper a patronisin gesture towards all that's best and most despised. The savage gentility, the abject smell-o-the-pew provincialism in the face of culture – takin the auld sense o that word – whether oor ain or o other lands. The quantity o communication, in inverse ratio to its quality. The Zeit withoot a Geist.

It's worse than evil: it's borin.

'Twas ever thus, did I say?

Let's look at the thusnesses. The century before the last one helps us here. In the stack room, almost thirty year back, I came across auld Kierkegaard, chunterin on aboot what to him was 'the present age' – 1846! – when everythin's left standin but is 'cunningly' emptied o meanin. What's left standin? Ruins? Well, I'm a ruin then, and must soon crumble.

A generation on, and Monsieur Flaubert is scratchin away in a letter to Gospodin Turgenev, November

1872. One structure's still miraculously intact then – the *cher maître*'s pavilion at Croisset, and productive o meanin, but. Presumptuous wee bastard that I am, I've worked over the salient part o auld Gus's scrieve to his Russian pal:

> I'd dearly love to write
>> In my ivory-towered halls,
> But a rising tide of shite
>> Is battering the walls.

So have we always lived in an Age of Shite? As the folk wisdom has it, 'Toalies aye float ti the top'? Ay, but what will change are the ingredients o the shite. And the big difference, the-day, is that all, ivory tower and all, have been utterly engulfed. Flaubert went on aboot the Age o *muflisme*. Me, I go on aboot the final triumph o oor Age of Shite.

Also sprach Herr Professor Doktor Torrance.

I'm better than borin: I'm evil.

What, or rather who, broke up oor Mikie and his Gayle?

The wee *clype* was punished.

Oh he was punished all right.

Burtie, he didnae deserve to go like that.

He didnae, anyway.

Nor did Mikie Bessop: found dead in his ward, aged 56. Cause of death given as: heart failure. I'd rather not say any more about that, or him.

What of the lady vanishèd, Miz' Dornacher von

Merrimon? Thon floozie shoulda been brought back for questionin. The hüre she was. She'll be an auld hüre now. I imagine her, predatory, itinerant, a one-woman perpetuity in all the states of the South: a blend of Blanche Du Bois and Gothic witch of the mountains, combustibly marinaded in moonshine. Wherever she is, let her broil.

Maybe I was her in a future life; or will be, in a past one. I've written mair o this account than you – or rather I – realise. The artist is *always* a liar – that's commonplace enough, but he's even mair o a hinter. Remember, too, that any narrator can be sae unreliable that ye cannae rely on him to be always unreliable. Besides, someone as theatrical as me plays many parts; efter all, I'm the bairn of a working-class couple who became nouveau riche, and at Mauletoun (and since) I've mingled wi the toffs. I've lived 'cross-wise', to quote H.G. Wells, through all the strata: I'm a sociological stravaiger, wi rare insights into hou baith the other halves live. My various arts – for a while – proved a nice wee earner. That in itself would probably have redeemed me in the eyes o my faither.

What of eaves-eyebrow'd Doctor Henry Baxendale, former and only headmaster of Mauletoun Preparatory School? In thae lang days, alternately tense and relaxed, when thon venture (under that name) was windin doun, he uttered many *bon mots*, maistly purloin'd from Shakespeare. He considered it incumbent upon himself to deliver manifold valedictory pronouncements, not least on the quarry where Burt had been found: 'O why should nature build so foul a den / Unless the gods delight in tragedies?' Nae doobt it had been some solace to him that, as well as his whisky collection, he might well have had access to the clinic's mair potent 'calming' substances – I'm speculatin, but as headmaster he probably had a spare key to the medicine cabinet. Like me, he ofttimes crept aboot the clinic, and to be fair I was grateful to him for his help in gettin me OFF GAMES.

Anyway, in thae last days he tried to ingratiate himself with his soon-to-be-ex-colleagues – 'I'll give you a glowing testimonial!' – but the only real rapport was in the relationship between the two dugs – his own and the Wilkies'. The two wee sowels were seen thegither, gambolling aboot in the paddock, sniffin each ither's erses, two at least of the school's dramatis personae intent on enjoying (as Karl Marx says somewhere) an 'orgy of reconciliation'.

Baxo himself found further solace in the airms o one o the parents, Mrs Anthea Ross-Lithgow, a rich and sonsie widow of forty-five. We kent he'd been cairryin-on wi her long before Mr Torquil Ross-Lithgow was suddenly defeated by his habits of corpulence; at home matches where, as ye ken, parents could visit the school for the afternoon, one of the boys (not me – honest) caught Anthea and her ripe swain a-makin 'the-beast-with-two-backs' at Wallace's Well. Good job Gayle and Michael werenae also deployin that bower at the same time – two's company, four's communism – and as well, too, that Mr Hamish Strang wasnae in the vicinity o their capers. He'd have been brandishin his Bible like there was no tomorrow, which for that apocalyptic gentleman there probably wasn't.

So Baxendale was after all able to take an early and secure retirement. No star-cross'd lover he. The Ross-Lithgow loot enabled him to take out annual season tickets for the Shakespeare Memorial Theatre (as it still was) in Stratford-upon-Avon. His bride accompanied him on these pleasant séjours. He could bray with the pick of them in the theatre bar, as if a myriad of Bottoms had indeed gone up in the world, or at least in a simulacrum of that world – or as he'd have pit it, via Will, 'the best in this kind are but shadows'. Sure, Mrs Ross-Lithgow-Baxendale had an unTitania-like tendency to snore, if still refinedly, during the performances, but to her credit she would wake up every time Lady Macbeth shrieked, 'Out, damned spot!'

(All that Shakespeare! And yet Baxendale reminded o nothin sae much as *Götterdämmerung*'s Hagen as played by Mephistopheles.)

Yer man (as me Irish grannie would say) made his final bow no many years efter, cirrhosis-liver'd, an outgoing Prospero dismissing his shades. Cheerio, Baxio. Nothing in your life became you like the leaving it. I can imagine.

Mind you, there's a wee postscript, or raither EPILOGUE no less. Baxendale and the trembling-digited dentist, Mr Airchie Thomson, had been fellow-members of the Auchtermyre Business and Professional Men's Club, weill-kent for their good-humoured and well-lubricated eloquence on speakers' night. I aye thought there was something between these two.

What if, thegither, they had contrived (via a deliberate dental cock-up) that the body at the quarry wasnae Burt but thon other laddie that went missin at the time? Come to think of it, could Burt still be alive? Was that pear-headed, orange-coloured sexagenarian I saw in the Glesca Shoogle the other day, comin oot o St Enoch, was that Burt?

No. It cannae be. The only remainin trace o him is that great stone face of him at the quarry. It still scares the shite oot o those who venture there. Yet ye only see it at a particular angle; move your heid by one degree, it vanishes, and it's just an auld, lang-disused quarry again; very Cézanne, very Cubist, if I may say so. You can carry on enjoying your picnic there, or whatever else ye get up to *sur l'herbe*.

Let the poor bugger rest. In bone or stone. Och weill.

Durin these last days at Mauletoun, Captain Wilkie asked after me: what were my plans? *University, sir,* I said, and he smiled. His faither had wanted him to become a professor of art history like himself, but the interest wasnae there. He wanted action, based on exact science, and ran away to sea.

'So you see, Torrance. Believe it or not, I was a rebel, like you.'

He put a hand on my shouther: the first and last time he did that.

'But I'm getting older, Torrance; my life is about to change; my work here has to end sometime. I'd've wished it otherwise – the work, that is; the other change is more personal, it's welcome, even overdue … I've tried to do my best by you lads. It's a world of hard knocks: I've received them and' – with an uncharacteristically sarcasm-free chuckle – 'I may even have administered them. I wanted to prepare you chaps for that world. Tough love, you might call it. I thought even Andy Burt might benefit from it; I was wrong.

'I'm getting older, and as I say my life must change direction: well, you might as well know if you don't already, and you probably do, dammit – I'll soon be a father of one, rather than a father of many on a ship or in a school. I don't understand art – you'll have to forgive me for that – but I know that … there's something else beyond – ' (He pointed in all directions) ' – all that anger, all that waste out there.

'Wish me well, Torrance, as I wish you well.'

He shook my hand and I saw him no more. I found oot later that he and his missus did efter all stay on at Mauletoun / Crockarkie, long after what he'd planned, and to the bitter end. The couple probably needed stability and distraction at that time. For word reached me, through university contacts, that his Molly's baby had been stillborn. Like the Malorys, they would never become parents. The Wilkies remained great dog lovers, enterin their charges at shows, winnin rosettes. Norrie Wilkie at last entered a university – Aberdeen – to study for a diploma in divinity: he wanted to become a minister o the Church o Scotland. A friend o mine there had tea wi him in his room at Crombie Hall of Residence – I can imagine Wilkie there, his trimmed, spade-like naval beard in profile, complainin to my friend that this room was smaller than a ship's cabin, its window meaner than a porthole. I was telt that Wilkie was lonely if kindly among thae young folk of the '70s. He disapproved o their socialism, their liberalism, what have you, but he listened to them wi interest and respect: they were there to learn, and so was he.

My friend – nou a weill-kent poet – had clearly provided Wilkie wi the unlikely company he craved. But the captain missed his Molly terribly, and left Aberdeen efter only one semester. He resumed his lecturin post at the Naval College, and on retirement he and Molly bought a derelict farmhouse just outside Dunkeld; spruced it up; enjoyed walkin their dugs in the surroundin woods and hills. They must hae kent Birnam and Dunsinane better than Baxendale ever did. I pieced thegither much o their later life from the internet – no everyone from Mauletoun left such an electronic trail, and maist left nane at all – and I learned that they baith lived weill into their nineties, receivin auld guests from maritime and canine days, forby followin new Zeitgeists with increasing puzzlement.

As I was fillin my trunk wi the remainin contents o my neuk o the dormitory cupboard, Cathy Malory entered, and looked at me quizzically. She wore her habitually worried, concerned expression, but this time it was all withoot words. The old banter between us had somehow ceased, and she left that vast depopulatin room. She and her motherly ways were already fadin from my life.

I heard a faint 'goodbye' as she descended the grand stair o Mauletoun Hoose.

As I grew older, I remembered her singin. It was whenever I passed the Malorys' door that I could hear her entertainin Peter wi songs she had picked up as a bairn in the miners' rows, as a farm lass in the various parts o the county, coastal and inland, as a young nurse doin her rounds. You understand that the details come from what I learned later: at Mauletoun, while I loved her soothin, protective voice, I didnae care for the songs. To me, they werenae classical (yet I worshipped Janáček and Bartók!), and at that time – prig that I was – I lumped everythin non-classical as the kind o kitsch my faither sang as he shaved.

But nou I remember – though I thought it odd at the time (which is nae doobt why I remember) – that

Cathy once telt me that it was only efter the death o her ain mother that she understood the meanin o the word 'motherland'. It was only much later that I could understand (and appreciate) what she meant by that.

Her songs were those o 'Fife and all the lands aboot it', as the line goes: all part o the 'carrying stream' of folk tradition. Sometimes you'd hear Mrs Makarowski jynin in when the twa women were thegither in the kitchen. I've since wondered if Mrs Makarowski blended such songs wi ony Polish ones taught her by her man ... an idle fantasy, mebbe: I hae learned, though, that a good number o pieces in Cathy's repertoire were local adaptations, often in the county's dialects, o ballads, catches, nursery rhymes from across central Europe – variously sinister, comic, tender.

I could surmise – again from later knowledge o the Malorys – that Cathy's lore would be invaluable to her man as he worked on his Fellowship thesis. It was a study that he thought he'd never complete. The loss o Burt, the impendin retirement, left him wi time emptied o responsibility but filled wi lament: he could get through his hours wi a painstakin resolution o his ethnological pursuits.

And of course there were nou mair opportunities to stay wi Neil and his family. Peter could sound out his nephew on research methods. At last, too, the family (including the lassies, while they were still bairns) could visit Scotland and occupy rooms in the ample cottage taken by Cathy and Peter just a few miles east o Lettermuchill, in the village o Wester Cadham. This final dwellin o the Malorys was perched at the top o the brae, where the long street from the main road rises to the secluded clachan. Peter could nou work at his desk, lookin oot on the triangular green and across to the hills at the other side o the howe. As they were still sae near to Mauletoun, the old Colonel – accordin to his diaries, in Neil's possession – would retrace the Sunday walks he had led wi the boys and would stand quietly by the quarry. For all its associations, this was a landscape and a land that was his wife's, and that he, an Englishman, had come to love.

I've even found myself in the School o Scottish Studies in Edinburgh, where they hae recordins o Cathy wi her songs, and a copy o Peter's thesis. Here was an archive, I felt, that even the-day should be on everybody's lips, at least hereaboots.

Now and then Cathy and Peter were able to travel doun to the State Hospital at Dunarty, where – under conditions of strictest security – they were allowed to visit Michael Bessop. Every time they approached that high, barbed-wire fence they felt apprehensive. They could not, of course, be alone with Michael: these were not nurses, observed Cathy to Peter, like herself and her former colleagues.

Michael's babbles became increasinly incomprehensible. There were times when he grat, and the tears mingled wi the dribblins from his slackened mouth. Cathy wanted to hug him, but was warned off. The couple persisted wi their visits, but the experience became mair and mair harrowin: thon's clear from Peter's diaries.

What's less clear is as follows. It was in an earlier and mair conventional hospital that, thirty year earlier, Peter had first met Cathy. At Queen Margaret in Dunfermline, she was a trainee nurse and he was a junior doctor (ay, that's right – a doctor!): such encounters, they say, are clichéd, but that's because, well, they were frequent. Cathy and Peter, however, were uncommon people in a common situation. She was a working-class lassie, bright, warm, and o quiet, understated passion. Efter his years at the Staff College at Albury, Peter had gone on to study medicine: his life, ye could say, was a series o long pilgrimages. But he never cited his civilian clinical practice, or his relevant qualifications, in what today we'd cry his CV.

His diaries are therefore unrevealin on this side o his life: anely the barest facts are recorded. Had he been subject to parental pressure from his upper-middle-class Surrey family, constantly required to achieve as much as his cleverer sisters? In his letters – and mair recently his e-mails – Neil has speculated on this: 'Grandfather Humphrey and Grandmother Olivia were a formidable pair, cold, unforgiving – they thought that Peter, as their only son, had married beneath him.'

It's on the record that as regards his war-time gallantry in Burma, when he rescued and restored to life a good many o his brothers-in-arms, he put that doun to his military rather than his medical expertise. Neil has suggested that he had witnessed the aftermath o atrocities – comrades beheaded by the Japanese invaders, wounds so horrific they were untreatable, all leadin to a sense o failure on his part, compounded by survivors' guilt.

He simply felt, it seems, that he wasnae a good enough doctor, would tak absolutely nae credit for any successes, and refused to list his medical qualifications in any accounts of his career. At Mauletoun ye suspect that he would aye defer to the opinions o Cathy, Dr Davidson, and even Gayle, in cases o illness and injury among the boys. Whatever the full reasons for his reticence on this side o his multi-faceted life, ye could at least understand his empathy for the deeply (and similarly?) troubled Bessop.

Peter seems to have regained his self-confidence wi his next self-reinvention. At Albury he had developed a strong interest in history; mythology and anthropology went into the mix, and literature – especially poetry, the soldier's art as we ken – had aye been a source for him o both solace and galvanisation. So when, around 1957, the posts of senior nurse and senior history teacher at Mauletoun were advertised, they attracted successful applications from Cathy and Peter respectively. The couple were ready for a calmer, mair rural environment within the county: Cathy especially, for all her proletarian loyalties, wasnae over-romantic aboot grime and machinery and arguin wi relatives aboot recent events in Hungary. As for Peter, he was a man who had been in the thick o destructive forces for much o his youth. He was all the mair determined to spend the rest o his life on whatever was constructive. The guidance o young folk towards their maximum fulfilment appeared to be the ideal outlet for him.

And then the Malorys found that they had, in a sense, adopted two vulnerable folk, a bairn cried Burt and a young man cried Bessop, baith o whom they would ultimately lose.

So much for the information that could be retrospectively gathered in recent years, no least because of you, Neil, if I can now address you directly in the course of this scrieve. I'm writin this in 1999, when I'm no yet fifty, and wonderin just hou much or rather hou little o the new millennium I'll be able to witness.

But for the sake o you readers generally – and no least you, Muriel - I can tell ye that memory has been filled oot by meetin Neil Malory Gomshall at an international conference on folklore at Glasgow University; I'd been invited to sing at it. His affiliation was cited as the Rijksmuseum. Given that Malory isnae a common name, and that I'd kent that Cathy and Peter holidayed in Holland, I plucked up the courage to ask him if he … And so our conversations, thae diaries o Peter's that he made available to me, the tantalisin if scant details available on the web: they enabled me to reconstruct a past I'd lived through only as an intellectually precocious and emotionally immature twelve-thirteen-fourteen year old in the early 1960s.

Neil: this screed approaches its end, and I myself might no be far behind. I'll be postin it to you in Amsterdam and I ask you – when she's ready – to make it and other documents available to my god-daughter and heiress Muriel. I want her to know everything – well, just about everything: I'll leave her to infer the rest.

I thank you, Neil, for your part in our exchange of documents and other information. I must now tell you that while the Glasgow conference was the first occasion when I met you, it wasn't the first time I saw you.

I had been working for a few years during the early '80s in Edinburgh, as a research assistant in the library of the Art College. It was ideal: a bit of a sinecure, really. I commuted from Scoonie, where my parents' not unwelcome demises had left me with their art deco pile on the main road towards Silverburn and Lundin Links. A long commute, many would say, but I never tired of the views of the Forth estuary and the Lammermuirs beyond.

Neil, you've since told me that Cathy died shortly before her seventieth birthday, of breast cancer. She – and for that matter Peter – would have known only too well what was happening inside her. But I digress. A little.

One morning – it must have been late August of 1984 – I was waiting for my train to the capital. A couple was preparing to board, and they appeared to be bound for a flight as they had a good bit of luggage, and the woman – the lady - spoke with an accent: Belgian or Dutch, I thought. Then I noticed a distinguished, silver-haired old gentlemen with them, speaking in a voice that sounded familiarly rich and mellow, if now rather halting, and at times even a little cracked.

I thought – is it him? Peter Malory, after all these years? Should I go up and say hello, reintroduce myself as ... then a voice within me said: no, it may not be him, you're imagining things, he wouldn't remember you anyway, perhaps ... The train arrived.

The old man stepped back as the couple – and I – boarded. I saw him waving to his friends. They were in late middle age, but still youthful; the elderly gentleman, whoever he was, must have been a commanding presence in his time, but now he was a little stooped. There was an expression of great sadness on his face. Just as well I didn't intrude, I thought. Yes – it's definitely Colonel Peter Malory, but this is a private matter for him. He's seeing off his friends, his family, for the last time. A silly little boy from Mauletoun has no part in this.

The train was off, the platform receded, and that was it. I dared not sit near the couple – I don't quite know why – and did not see the husband again until I came up to you, Neil, at the Glasgow conference.

When I so fleetingly saw the Colonel - Peter - for that last time at Kirkcaldy station I had an inkling that his doom, his weird was upon him, and that he knew it. I hope, Neil, you won't mind me putting it like that. The folklorist in him, I like to think, might have used the same expression.

Neil: I know my own weird is upon me.

At this time of writing, my god-daughter Muriel knows nothing of my records and yours. She's too young to be concerned with these: let her concentrate on her studies. I want her to work, wait and hope.

In a few years, though, she'll be curious about the strange creature who cared for her after the deaths of John and Nicol, and about the 'Burt-Bessop case', whose facts or fictions were 'kindly and unfairly tried / By a squalor of honest men', and with which that strange creature was mair than a wee bit acquainted. By the time you contact her (to her, it'll be out of the blue) she'll already be on the trail – I know that budding intellectual curiosity of hers.

How, you may ask, did Mr Billy Torrance – the idle aesthete who grew into an accomplished operatic and Lieder baritone, forby lauded exhibitor of neo-expressionist landscapes – acquire responsibility for this young lady Muriel Redburn? She was born in 1982 to a Dundee family with a history of what we now call substance abuse. It pains me even now, to think of that bairn in the filth of a Hilltown tenement.

John Antonelli and Nicol Tulloch were my closest friends – platonic to me if not to each other – at Glasgow University. I'd introduced them to each other and they loved me for that. The three of us became involved in gay activism on the campus and in the city. I came to regard them as my brothers – it was like that for someone who'd been an only bairn. They were blessed with a stable relationship such as I'd never experienced – one failed partner after another for me, I'm afraid – and dearly wanted to become adoptive parents. This was becoming a possibility in these times, and especially in the liberal milieu of Byres Road.

John had survived a strict Catholic upbringing, and Nicol an equally strict Presbyterian counterpart. There was much to redeem, you might say (as, in different contexts, for me ...) It was when Nicol was pursuing a postgraduate course in Dundee that he learned of the 'problem' family, and so it came about that Muriel joined us in Glasgow: I became in turn a sort of uncle figure, ideal for the godfaither role which John and Nicol wanted for me. (As for my loot, ye cannae tak it wi ye, as they say, but that hardly bothers me ...)

There was a lot of confused talk about class and gender at the time, not always along clear left-right lines: yet dogmatism, as always, was trying to muscle love out of its path. That, though, was a petty irritation for my two friends, compared to what would follow for them. Muriel was only twelve when John and Nicol were set upon by a coalition of Rangers and Celtic supporters intent on making common cause against perceived threats to Christian and family values.

It happened not far from Kelvingrove, at the angle of Sauchiehall and Argyle Streets, down a nearby close where my two friends had been dragged. They were repeatedly stabbed and their skulls were crushed by metal bars. They died in the ambulance. The thugs had dispersed by the time the police reached the scene, but in due course they were able to resume their traditional rivalry behind the walls of Barlinnie.

I'd been mindin Muriel that evenin, to let my two friends spend some time thegither as a couple at an Indian restaurant and a concert. The polis - police - knock on my door marked the beginnin of the last phase of my life.

And so, Neil, I've telt – told – it as it was, or sae it seemed to me. I hope you'll no think too badly of me.

7

A LAST VIEW OF THE BIG HOOSE

What a kindly old man he is after all, thinks Muriel, as she recalls the invitation from Professor Neil Malory Gomshall: *Do please come over with your little boy; it would be lovely for us to have a child running about again in Van Tasselstraat. My wife is looking forward to meeting you: you'll have her life-story out of her, I'm sure.*

The Professor's a renowned curator, historian and – since his retirement – has found a lucrative career as a notoriously sensationalist novelist, writing under a pseudonym, and translated into goodness knows how many languages! So much she has gathered from the breathless style of his messages. He sounds fun, really: he'll entertain the wee one with his tales – the ones suitable for children, that is.

Muriel had hoped to fly from Aberdeen but only Edinburgh-Schiphol was available: never mind, it has been a poignant, if expensive, trip south by train. At the Cupar stop, she has felt near to the mysterious past of her godfather. *On the other side of the water, thanks to the Professor, all will become clear. It will be good to sound him out in person: the e-mailed messages and documents can go only so far, and there is all that unique material which he can put at my disposal at his house beside the canal. The very sound of the Professor's voice: what a connection that*

*will be ... to those people, long dead, who featured in the life
of dear Billy, who has himself gone forth.*

Arrived at Edinburgh Airport, Muriel takes the
hand of her small Andrew: he's excited at this first
adventure, in a plane, to another country.

The flight path will be northerly before it turns east
and south-east towards Amsterdam. *I wonder,* Muriel
thinks aloud. – *What is it, Mummy? – It's a place down
there that Mummy knows, darling.*

Through thin clouds Muriel can clearly make out
Mauletoun House and all the lands about it. She
peers below, and is that the lady of the manor, Aileen
Burlington, walking her dogs from the main entrance?
Aileen, not as formidably posh as she had feared, had
been helpful down there, as helpful as she could have
been among that chaos of books, ledgers, bound and
loose journals, papers dog-eared, mouse-eaten and
decayed ...

The clouds thicken, Mauletoun disappears, she can
make out the coast, the North Sea, and soon after,
another coast ... Andrew has dozed off, as bairns do.
Half an hour before landing, his mother does likewise,
and dreams that ghosts are waving to her, friendly-
like, concerned ...

*Lavigny, Vaud, Switzerland, May 2012 – Kirkcaldy,
Fife, Scotland, April 2013*

GLOSSARY

A

aa all
aareadies already
aathin everything
aff off
afore before
ain own
aince once
alane alone
amang among
athort across
atween between
auld yins parents
awa away
awfy awful
aye always
ayont beyond

B

bade stayed
bauchle an old, useless,
  worn-out person
bi 's by his
blaw blow
blethering idle chatter
bluid blood
bore hole, opening, space between
bother tease, torment, wind up
brae slope; track or road up and down a slope
brak break
brekkin breaking
brig bridge

brither brother
burn stream, creek
burnside by the **burn** or stream; the waterside
Buroo the dole, unemployment / welfare payment;
  government office which issues the dole and which has a
  reputation for hassling claimants
byde remain, stay

C

cairn pile of stones, gathered together at
the summit of a hill or mountain by those who
have reached it
caum calm
chuckies pebbles, stones
clachan a (remote) group of buildings, a settlement not big
  enough to be called a village
claes clothes
clype a tell-tale, a grass
contermacious perverse, contrary
coort court
coos' cows'
corbie-stepped crow-stepped: aspect of traditional
  Fife domestic architecture, on gables
corp corpse, body
cowp refuse tip, rubbish heap
cuid could

D

dae do
deed aye indeed yes / always
den narrow valley with small river or stream, usually
  wooded and often with a gorge: a common feature in
  Fife
didnae didn't
dochters daughters
doo dove
drabbly, drabblichy showery, drizzly

droukit soaked, drenched
drouned drowned
drowie misty, drizzly, damp
drumlie cloudy, muddy, miserable
dugs dogs
dule-tree gallows
düne done
dunt blow, hit

E

ee eye
efter after
erse arse

F

faither father
fash worry
fause false
ferlie wonder, marvel
fin find
flouer flower
flutherin fluttering
forby moreover, as well as
foust, foustieness mustiness
frae from
fresh-flutherin fresh-fluttering

G

gairden garden
gaire part of a garment, by the knee
gang (aff) go off
gars makes, causes
gaun gone, going
gey very
gien gave
gleg quick, ready

gowpin gulping, swallowing
greet(in) cry(ing), weep(ing)
growes grows
grue horror
guidman, guidwife good man, good wife; ordinary decent
  folk

H

haar thick mist or fog of the east coast of Scotland
hauf-mirk half-darkness
haufwey half way
heid head
hit's it's
hingin oot hanging out
Holy-Joe [noun, here used adjectivally] an over-pious,
  sanctimonious, priggish person
hoose house
howffs pubs
hullocks hillocks
hüre whore

I

ilk, ilka each, every
ither other

J

jawed chattered, blethered
jessie a cissy / sissy; a weak, effeminate male
jo sweetheart, lover
jynin joining

K

keeks glances
keelies working-class males of cities (mainly Glasgow)

and assumed to be in trouble with the law
ken? you know what I'm saying? (**ken** – know)
kent knew

L

lang long
lauchter laughter
lawd lad
lee-lang whole, live-long
lichts lights

M

mair more
mairrit married
maist most
manky disgusting, in a filthy condition
maun must
mebbe maybe
mental crazy
mischancit unlucky
mither mother
Morlock one of the subterranean race, the Morlocks, in
    H.G. Wells's *The Time Machine*; term of abuse for a
    working-class person
mortal drunk
muckle big
murther murder
mustae must have

N

naebody nobody
neeps turnips
neuk corner
nou now
nourice nurse

O

onyhin anything
oor hour
ower over

P

pads paths
pettit petted
pit put
pit-on put-on, faked
port gate
prep the period for private study for pupils at a boarding
  school
puir poor
puir-bit thing poor little thing

R

reek smoke
reesle rustle
richt right
rouch rough

S

sae so
sang song
sapple foam; also onomatopoeic, suggesting the sound of
  water in movement
sclimmed climbed
scrieve a piece of writing; to write
selt sold
send message
shair sure
Shoogle the Glasgow subway / metro [from the verb
shoogle,
  to shake]

shouther shoulder

sitooterie an area with seats at the back of a house, in the garden (US: yard), where you can **sit oot**, sit out

snaw snow

snichered sniggered, giggled, laughed mischievously

snod comfortable, snug

sonsie buxom

souch breeze

sowel soul

stauns stands

stravaiger wanderer, traveller, itinerant

T

taen taken

tap top

thae those

thegither together

thocht thought

thon that

toalies turds

U

Unco Guid the godly, respectable folk free of sin (or who don't get caught) and who sit in judgment on others

V

verra very

W

wan one

warld world

wasnae wasn't

watter water

wean child [pronounced *wane*; conflation of **wee** and **ane** (one)]

weill-favoured handsome
weill-kent well-known
weird [as a noun:] a personal fate or destiny
wey way
whins gorse
whippitie-stourie a nimble person, light of foot
whitna what (not)
wirselves ourselves
wisnae wasn't
wog racist term of abuse directed at Asian people or even whites who have spent a long time in the East and whose skin has darkened. Sometimes cited as an acronym of *Wily Oriental Gentleman*

Y

yins ones
yuise use

ABOUT THE AUTHOR

Tom Hubbard is a Scottish novelist, poet and itinerant scholar who has worked in many countries. His permanent home is in his native Fife. He has been a Visiting Professor at the Universities of Budapest (ELTE), Connecticut (where he was Lynn Wood Neag Distinguished Visiting Professor of Scottish Literature in 2011) and Grenoble (as Professeur invité), and a Writer in Residence at the Château de Lavigny in Switzerland. His short book *The Integrative Vision: Poetry and the Visual Arts in Baudelaire, Rilke and MacDiarmid* (1997) was based on lectures to students of design at Glasgow School of Art. He was the first Librarian of the Scottish Poetry Library, from 1984 to 1992. His first novel *Marie B.* (Ravenscraig Press, 2008), based on the life of the Ukrainian-born painter Marie Bashkirtseff, was longlisted for a Saltire Society book award. His recent book-length poetry collections are *The Chagall Winnocks* (2011) and *Parapets and Labyrinths* (2013), both from Grace Note Publications, as well as a pamphlet collection, *The Nyaff* (2012), from Windfall Books of Kelty, Fife. An essay on the Scottish poet Harvey Holton (1949-2010) was published as a pamphlet by Fras Publications as *Harvey Holton: Bard, Makar, Shaman* (2013). He has edited a volume of essays, *The Poetry of Baudelaire*, which will appear from the New York publisher Grey House in 2014. He has also recently made English and Scots versions of poems by the nineteenth-century Russian poet Lermontov for an anthology *After Lermontov*, edited by Peter France and Robyn Marsack (Carcanet 2014). He is on the editorial board of the journal *Scottish Affairs*, and an honorary visiting fellow at the University of Edinburgh Institute of Governance, where he is working on a "Scotland and Europe" project with Dr Eberhard Bort.

Between 2000 and 2010 he was research fellow and editor of major bibliographical projects: BOSLIT (the Bibliography of Scottish Literature in Translation, University of Edinburgh and the National Library of Scotland, at http://boslit.nls.uk [2000-2005]), and BILC (the Bibliography of Irish Literary Criticism, National University of Ireland Maynooth, at http://bilc.nuim.ie [2006-2010]).

The Lucky Charm of Major Bessop is Tom Hubbard's second novel.